THE PHANTOM KEEPER

AMANDA FERREIRA

THE PHANTOM KEEPER

Cover design and chapter header design by Selkkie Designs – www.selkkiedesigns.com

Interior formatting by Leslie Copeland

Character art by Svifian8 on Twitter/X, Bluesky, and Instagram

First edition: September 2025

ISBN 9781778217432 (ebook)

ISBN 9781778217425 (paperback)

To my boys, Grayson and Milo,
who light up my life.
And to Nick, who believed.

BOOKS BY AMANDA FERREIRA

Entangled with an Elf Prince

A Chronicle of Monsters (Anthology)

AUTHOR'S NOTE

The Phantom Keeper is a slowburn adult romantic fantasy featuring a trans protagonist and a male love interest. While I've tried to write the book's nuances with sensitivity and care, it contains subject matter which might be upsetting to some readers. This includes: implied deadnaming, misgendering, body dysmorphia, disfigurement, PTSD, depictions of a cult (in the past), brief mentions of child abuse (in flashbacks), brief mentions of suicidal thoughts (in the past), fantasy violence, and descriptive sexual situations between two consenting adults.

CHAPTER ONE

I've come to anticipate these late-night knocks on my bedroom door. Short, sharp, and sudden, they never wake me—I'm rarely asleep at this hour—but they always wake Hadrian; he stirs at my side, his bed pushed flush against mine, the floor of our shared room marred by the teleportation circle I've been drawing on the stones for the past two days.

"You just got comfortable," he whispers, barely peeking open one of his eyes. I'd crawled into bed only a moment ago, my vision blurry, my body exhausted, but how he noticed is beyond me; a lion-shifter by birth and a fire mage by trade, Hadrian holds an arsenal of light, power, strength, and fury between his ribs, but he sleeps like the dead. "Don't go."

"I thought you liked these adventures," I chide, and a deep rumble shakes from his chest. Even wrapped in shadow, his broad shoulders, square jaw, and long legs cut a distinct silhouette. "You're half the reason I even agree to these."

"I'm not," he mumbles as the knock comes again, more

insistent this time. Three raps. Four. He drapes an arm over his eyes, anticipating the blazing torchlight from the hall. "Am I?"

I could lie, but Hadrian's always been kind to me; assigned to share my room these past eight years, he could've resented the space I've taken up, the books I've piled on every shelf, the potions I've mixed and long abandoned on the floor, but he's never minded. Giving him a reason—a paid reason especially—to leave the academy for a few weeks at a time is often the only thing I can do to repay him, so I reply, "It's the least I can do," and I mean it.

Crossing the room to the door, I slip on a dark blue robe with the academy insignia stitched across the chest, the expensive fabric embroidered in black, red, and gold. It feels as heavy as lead when I'm as tired as I am, and it takes me far too long to realize I've grabbed Hadrian's, not my own; it smells like the concoction he rubs in his hair when he bathes.

My hands are stiff from the hours I've spent on the floor, my fingers hardly closing around the door handle. I wasn't careful; behind me, I can see the lines, circles, and patterns of my design, the rune paint a shimmering white in the darkness. I should've covered everything before going to bed, but I can't do it now.

With a groan, I pull open the door on its ancient hinges, my foot all that keeps it from slamming shut again, the draft from the hall ruffling my hair. For a student dormitory, all the rooms here are protected like vaults, the timber thick and enchanted, the frames and doorknobs iron to deter fae.

On the other side, cast in orange and gold, stands the academy's headmaster, her robes shining in the light from the torch at her back, the open flame mounted high on the wall. It will burn and burn, some say, until the end of time; all the fires here are magical, anchored to the will of a god.

"You're awake," she says, and she seems genuinely relieved. But the emotion passes quickly, and irritation appears in the lines around her eyes and mouth. "You kept me waiting."

"I assumed you'd rather not see me in my under-clothes," I reply, but the attempt at lightening her mood is met with silence. She raises a brow, her dark bangs sweeping across her eyes, almost masking her.

We are *not* friends, the headmaster and I. She makes it no secret that she tolerates me at best and happily exploits me at worst, my skill set uniquely...profitable.

"A mine has collapsed," she says with seriousness, at last revealing why she's come. "Seventeen hundred miles from here, on the continent."

I nod. "It can't well have been nearby," I point out. After all, the Academy of Light sits atop four floating isles, each chained to the world below like a ship to the bottom of the sea. But this retort earns yet another raised brow from her, and I clear my throat, inclining my head as if to apologize and acknowledge her status, several tiers above anything I've so far achieved on my own. Though she's only two decades or so older than me, the golden knots pinned to her right shoulder denounce her high rank as a scholar and mage, as a teacher and philosopher. Her role as headmaster is one I've dreamed of seizing from her since the moment I first arrived here eleven years ago.

"There were dozens of lives lost, perhaps more," she says, stressing the horror of the accident, but in truth, the details hardly matter to either of us; one dead or a hundred dead often pays the same. "The grieving families have written for weeks, claiming that despite their pleas, no phantom keepers have

3

come. They beg for your help. They say they can hear the dead wail." She looks away suddenly, just slightly, her eyes flicking to the right, as if she's disturbed by the mere idea of death, as if all lost souls trapped on this plane don't call out when they discover they're still here, unable to pass on. "Will you go?"

I can't, I want to say, but it's an old habit; an inkling from my old life where I didn't lie as easily or as readily as I do now. *I stole the title of phantom keeper. I know only a handful of spells necessary for the work.* But it's more than enough, so I make the effort to bury the truth. "Have they sent the funds for more rune paint? I have little remaining in the allotment you last requisitioned for me."

She purses her lips, unable to hide the glint of disappointment that streaks across her face. "They've sent... enough," she says tersely, looking past my shoulder and into the room beyond. Hadrian hasn't moved, but I know she sees him there, his body sprawled atop the sheets in full view. They are shameless, it seems; I've never met a shifter unafraid to bare their skin. If his nakedness embarrasses her, however, she hides it well. "It will pay for your horse, fare aboard one of the merchant ships that comes to the island, but nothing more."

A paltry sum indeed. A few thousand feet below the isles is our only access point to the world beyond the academy: a small island with a harbour, which accepts deliveries from the continent of everything we can't produce here ourselves. I'm almost surprised she brought me the plea at all; I can only assume the academy is getting a very small cut of the fee. Humouring such a thing is hardly worth her time—or my own.

But when I think about the weeks of freedom, of the fresh, open air, of the countless phantoms I'll have access to,

I know my answer. Even if I had to work for free, I would take the job.

"Very well," I agree, and behind me, Hadrian grunts. "But I won't go alone."

The headmaster hesitates, though I know she can't be shocked; I always ask for company now, and Hadrian has proven he'll return with me when the job is done. But it always gives her pause. I'm a prize, after all; the academy's golden goose. And to lose me and Hadrian both if we're ambushed by monsters on the road...

Finally, she nods. "It will be arranged. You have five and a half weeks to return."

Based on the distance alone, I can guess where we're going—and the opportunity it presents. "Six," I insist, crossing my arms and resting my shoulder against the door. It threatens to crush all my bones, the weight immense. "It's only an extra three days."

Her nostrils flare. But she's conceded everything else thus far; why not this? "Six, then."

I nod, and as the door swings shut behind her, I turn back to face Hadrian, his eyes flashing open in the gloom of the room. They're piercing, as are the eyes of every mage; his and mine are the same, a bright, vibrant green—deep, dazzling, opalescent.

"You're lucky I like you," he says. "Six weeks of class is a lot to miss." But he's smiling, and that alone lights every corner of our room.

I laugh; I can't help it. "We leave at dawn tomorrow," I inform him, going to pack a few of my things in a satchel I always keep at the foot of my bed. Looking up, I catch him still watching me, his expression a little soft. "Try to find some trousers for the road if you can, yeah?"

~

The descent from the floating isles to the waterlogged island below takes three days. The gondolas are slow and manually cranked, a team of men and women paid expressly for the purpose of helping us fall from the sky with as much grace as possible.

Hadrian is pale the whole way down, gripping his seat across from me until his nails leave indentations in the cracked leather, the interior of the gondola hot and colourless from the years it's spent in the sun. "This is always the worst part," he says, too afraid to even look out the window at the sky above. "I don't know how you stand it."

"It's a necessary evil," I reply, and he shakes his head, then goes a little green around the edges of his face and buckles forward. I rub his arm to comfort him, a small consolation. "There's no other way."

And there isn't—not without plunging to certain death, our bones left to drift in the sea. Escape from the academy is made near impossible this way; everyone must use the gondolas, but to use the gondolas, the leave must be ordained. Sanctioned. Planned for.

No one knows, when they accept the invitation to study here, that there's no way out.

"Plus," I add cheerily, the emotion forced and entirely fake, "there was cargo."

Cargo, by which I mean the dozen boxes of books and scrolls crammed into the tiny gondola with us, the texts written by scribes and scholars in the upper echelons of the academy. These musings are our only export, besides mages for hire, the words meant to be disseminated across the far reaches of the continent; and in truth, *these* are what allow for any trip from the isles at all. But even then, other than us, I've never seen another mage leave the academy without armed guard.

"Let's go," I urge gently, the moment the doors can be opened on the next lowest of the isles, just as evening breaks over the sky on our first day of travel. Hadrian follows despite the tremor in his legs. He takes hold of my hand to steady himself, just for a moment, and I let him. Beneath my gloves, he can't see the spells I've painted on my skin, on the back of each hand: one for protection, one for disguise. I pray I won't need either.

At my back, I carry only one weapon—my bow, unstrung and oiled, the string wound in a small pouch at my side. My quiver dangles from my hip, each arrow carved and shaped with precision, the ends weighted with feathers. Hadrian carries nothing but his own skin, as he always does, and leaves our bags of supplies on the gondola. He's a weapon with just his fists, or when shifted, with every inch of his body.

On the second day of our earthbound travel, as the long seconds stretch from minutes to hours, Hadrian pulls me in close, the fire magic in his blood like a small hearth beneath his skin. "You will speak nothing of this," he says, and I laugh, his head buried in the curve of my shoulder, his eyes pressed to the crook of my neck. I almost consider him more than a friend in moments like these, since I allow the closeness. I welcome it.

He's the only person I've let share any part of my life since I destroyed everything I used to be.

On the morning of the fourth day, as we await the ship that will take us to the continent, we watch the sunrise from the sandy beach that frames the north side of the island. Out here, there's nothing but sea salt and sunlight, farmland

and animals, orchards and honeycombs. It's almost picturesque, when seen like this.

"We could stay out here," Hadrian says, our feet beneath the waves. The water is cool, the shoreline so shallow in the spot we've chosen that we could lie back in the surf and still breathe. "On the continent, I mean. The academy wouldn't search for us."

I can hear the words he can't quite say. It's true, but only because they wouldn't look for *him*. Hadrian is the son of an alpha, one day meant to lead a pride of lion-shifters in his father's stead. Like all the students imprisoned here, he's not allowed to leave the academy, in theory, but they can't stop him from failing to return. And he has no need to, now that he can control his fire magic.

"You could stay," I reply, the sand turning dark as the sun passes behind a cloud. "But they would send out demands for my return. Assuming they didn't just kill me."

This threat, of course, is how they control all the mages at the academy—beyond the trap of the floating isles themselves. On the day I enrolled here, the headmaster took a vial of my blood, and like a taunt, she keeps it with all the others in the room next to her office that has no other door besides the one by her desk. I can feel it thrumming there, sometimes; I can hear my own blood like a heartbeat through the walls, pounding dully against the stones. She could kill me with it, if she wished. I wouldn't be missed— not like Hadrian. To kill Hadrian would start a war.

"You could run with us," he offers, and his smile is easy. In the sun, his golden hair is almost a mane, the ends wild around his shoulders and face. "With my pride."

I turn away so I can pull on my boots. "That won't work. The academy would never accept that as a reason not to kill me."

8

"Marry me then," he says seriously. "Would they kill the husband of a king?" I stare at him, then kick a little sand over his legs. He adds, "We could use a talent like you."

A talent. It's a loaded word, but it's not unkind. I'm a phantom keeper, able to speak to the dead; I'm a lexicon mage, able to shape rune paint into spells; I'm a master marksman, able to hit any target, of any size, at any distance, with my bow.

But I'm also a long list of things he doesn't know. I'm a curse; I'm a killer. I'm a runaway. I'm a thief. And I'm a danger, a threat—even now—to all those who live and will ever live.

I hold out my hand to help him up. "The ship awaits," I say, sounding deeply unconvinced. I have no idea if the ship that has pulled into the harbour has come for us, if its pale sails are the mark of cabin space or room for cargo, but we can only find out. "Let's see what the future holds, shall we?"

CHAPTER TWO

In this tiny ship on the wide-open sea, Hadrian and I share a room with two bunks, each hardly wide enough to fit our shoulders. They're uncomfortable to sleep in, so we don't bother trying; we doze instead, a few hours here or there, on our pair of travelling cloaks bundled together on the floor.

While Hadrian rests, I paint on my arms. Long, swirling patterns turn into runes that almost look like letters, the lines bleeding together to form a language no one knows. I can almost read it, I think; I can almost understand. But there's no need to. The magic comes whether I understand it or not.

By the time we reach the coastline, only my back is left unpainted. I've drawn on my feet, my legs, my hips, my chest; each elbow, each wrist, the curves of my shoulders, and the dips of my throat—everything besides my face is covered. And in the sunlight, the rune paint catches in the glow and refracts, turning from white to silver, then from silver to molten lead.

Hadrian watches me dress, and each layer builds atop the next, my skin protected by linen bindings that lie flush against my body. These are followed by loose trousers, a tunic, and then robes. I could wear armour even over that, but the summer is hot and humid on the continent, and I have Hadrian to threaten passing pickpockets with.

"Could another mage paint your back?" he asks idly, watching as I secure my hood in place over my head. The sides of my neck are painted too, so I try to leave nothing visible. "There's so much space there. You could cast a dozen more spells."

Or extend the reach of one powerful spell, I consider, nodding. "It's possible, but requires a great deal of trust. Since you can't see what's there, the spell could easily be intended to kill you."

Hadrian wrinkles his nose, the edges of his mouth pulling up with the movement. Betrayal of this kind sits strangely in his understanding of the world, his pride a place where everyone works actively to protect each other. To sabotage a sister or a brother, a friend or even an enemy in this way is unheard of. Fights are fair in the place he comes from, outcomes drawn in blood, not deception.

"Would you trust me?" he asks suddenly. I regard him as he sits cross-legged on the floor of our tiny cabin, his muscular arms left exposed by the thin sash across his chest passing for a tunic, his expression open, his jaw lined with a rough length of stubble that encroaches on his lips. He's forthright and earnest and has been since we met; he wouldn't lie, even to ease my pain. He's a blunt, well-meaning, and honest protector, for all that I don't actually need him.

No is the truth; I wouldn't trust him or anyone with such a thing. But I say, "You? In an emergency, maybe. But don't let that get to your head—you don't know any spells. It wouldn't work."

He beams, my Hadrian. It pulls at an old ache inside me, buried deep in my chest. Before coming to the Academy of Light, before I'd been sold to the phantom keepers, before my mother had died and I'd heard my first ghost, I'd believed no one close to me could hurt me. But now I know anyone can turn—even Hadrian. Over what, I don't know; but eventually, I'll lose him. I'm certain of it.

Bounding up behind me as I disembark the ship, Hadrian's elation at being back on land makes his smile swell almost to breaking. He's loud when he's happy; he claps passing sailors on the arm to thank them for our voyage and tips liberally, flipping silver coins even to barkeeps at taverns who don't serve us beyond setting the fees for our rooms. Some nights, a week into our journey, this leads to extra drinks; other nights, it opens entire wings of empty inns for our stay, the choice of rooms entirely up to us.

It takes a long two and a half weeks to reach Frostborro, and after a combined four days on the lower isles, six days on the ship, and eight days on horseback, the city on the outskirts of the mines rises from the gloom with the air of a cemetery.

Grey houses, grey streets, and grey glass in all the windows...it's obvious the town is built from what's been pulled from those mines, the cheapest stone hardly worth selling at all. It's a risky way of life, but still, the people dig here. And die.

At the front gate, a man with a scar through his right eye admits us without a word. He can't have known who to expect, but he can see the magic that we carry in our eyes alone. Who else would come to this place on urgent business? He can guess who we are.

Hadrian and I ride carefully between the houses, a hollow feeling hanging over the black metal fences that surround the gardens and empty thoroughfares that criss-cross the streets. Businesses are rarely marked here; people hawk what they can sell through their own front doors. Every home could be a shop, every shop a home.

The mayor of Frostborro is a woman so young she looks around my age, a stone's throw from thirty, but her hair is entirely grey. Perhaps she uses dyes, a flare to earn respect. She meets us outside the courthouse, a stern-looking building that leans into the soil as if the ground is beginning to give way beneath it. How she knew we'd arrived, I'll never know.

Her mouth is pulled tight, her cheeks lined with both stress and grief. Her dark eyes, shadowed by a lack of sleep, linger on the academy crests branded onto our clothes. Hadrian really should be wearing his robes, but instead he's donned a loose-fitting tunic with a low neck, baring half his chest to the wind, his cloak marked instead with the academy's sigil across the back.

"Tell me you've come for the dead," she says, holding out her hands to take the bridles of our horses. We dismount quickly, aware of the lingering eyes from every house on the street. The people have been waiting, and they've grown impatient. Desperate. Needy. "Tell me this will be over soon."

I incline my head, my right arm crossed over my chest, the gesture formal and polite. "I just need two days to paint," I explain. "Then you'll have peace."

She weeps. It's so sudden, so automatic a response, it makes me wonder if she was likely to cry at any news at all. "Go," she says, pointing down the street at what I assume is her estate, the main building a large, hulking mass of grey stone and arched windows, the road winding straight up to her door. "Take any room. Paint your circle anywhere you like."

I usually prefer, for work like this, to draw the circle somewhere closer to the dead, but it'll do. Private, quiet, protected; I could ask for little more. "Thank you."

Hadrian follows me up to the door, hovering as I greet the waiting staff who have watched us approach from the long windows overlooking the front steps. They've arranged themselves in two neat rows inside the entryway, framing an ornate staircase that spirals up three floors. I take Hadrian's hand, urging him close. "Don't let them follow."

As he leans in to hear me, his breath plays along my face, the warmth of his skin like a balm to the iciness of my own. I run cold; I always have. But he burns like the sun.

At the base of the landing on the uppermost floor, Hadrian lingers at the lip of the stairs, keeping an eye on the people below. I start opening doors along either side of the hall, finding bedrooms, a room with a bath, a small library, and a room full of art. At the end, there's a room meant for weaving, the wools and wooden looms arranged along the walls. This will do.

It takes about an hour to clear the floor enough to work, then an hour more to arrange the paint I've brought where I expect to need it, dividing a small amount into a dozen tiny pots.

Arranging my hair is last. At this length, the ends just kiss the back of my neck, the black waves long enough to curl around my hand if I hold them in a fist. In my old life, I'd have been beaten for such an offense. Even now, my fingers shake as I tie it back, the mess held up with a length of string. I remind myself that no elder phantom keeper is coming to hold me down and shave my head, to bare my skin so someone else can paint above my ears, along my forehead, across my scalp, and over my eyes.

Raising both my hands, I cover my face. I should cut it, I know. I have no excuse for growing my hair as long as I have, for all that I lust for something more—for hair long enough to frame my face, to hide the width of my shoulders, to soften the harsh lines of my jaw...

Abruptly, I drop my hands. I don't have time to dream; not here. Not while there are people waiting for me. Counting on me.

Kneeling in the center of the room, I start to paint. One line becomes two, three becomes six. Eventually, seven empty pots become twelve.

I don't sleep. Hadrian visits me only once to bring me tea, holding the cup while I drink since I can't wash the paint from my fingertips. He sees the spells I've painted on the backs of my hands when he does.

"I would've protected you," he says, knowing only what the left sigil is for.

"I know," I reply. "It's for you."

It's a simple defensive spell, having to fit on so small a canvas. A shield spell, a bright burst of light between one person and some aggressor, to protect against an arrow, a sword slash, or a spear. Had we been ambushed and robbed, or attacked by some monster, it would hardly have helped, but I'd rather something than nothing.

Hadrian smiles gently in response, whispering my name. But it's not my name, what he says; not really. He only knows the name I'd offered him when we first met, the one my father had given me at birth. But it holds no truth for me anymore, and I don't hear it when he says it. "You think of everything."

"I try," I say with a laugh, and my gaze drifts to my bow

propped up against the wall, always in sight. "Will you rest tonight?"

"Maybe some," he says. "Against the door, so no one bothers you." *So no one sees the runes* is what he means, I assume.

The teleportation circle and the spells within have been a closely guarded secret for almost a thousand years, passed down from generation to generation of phantom keeper. No one knows what the runes mean or where the circles take the dead, but phantoms are always drawn there, and when they enter, none return. The magic works for no one but them.

When I can think of no other way to thank him, I touch Hadrian's forehead with my own. The contact is momentary, affectionate, like how one shifter would speak to another while shifted. It always makes him blush. "When this is over, we can travel to see the headlands," I promise him. "We can spare one day. The headmaster gave us leave for six weeks."

Hadrian closes his eyes. Breathes in. He won't ask what I know he wants to: if he can visit his pride. See his family. The problem is that six weeks isn't enough to search for them and return to the academy before they snap the vial of my blood and stop my heart. For all that I am valuable, the secrets I carry of the academy's are more so. They think there are others—other phantom keepers. If they knew I was the last, they would never dare hurt me. But it's a secret only I know.

"I'd like to see them," he says, and the phrasing is delicate, loaded. "But I won't risk your life."

Neither will I—not when my one life is all I have, and there's so much left for me to do. But I say, "If we can, we will."

Hadrian nods. "Do you want more tea?" he asks, the empty cup still in his hand.

I look up. He's so close that he's barely a hairsbreadth from kissing me. I've thought of it, in the past. But I know him—he'd want more. More of my time, more of my life, more of my secrets. And I can't let anyone get that close.

I pull away, shaking my head. "After the circle is done." I glance back at it, at what he could see of the room if he raised his head to look. But he never does. Even when I was painting the floor of our room back at the academy, he was always careful to avert his gaze. I don't know what I've done to deserve such a friend as he's been to me for so long.

Hadrian's eyes linger on my face before he shuts the door behind him. "Call me if you need me," he says, and is gone.

CHAPTER THREE

When the teleportation circle is finally complete, the last rune drawn under my thumb and forefinger, I come alive. Bright and glorious, the corresponding spell on my body thrums like a living thing, the location of the circle pulling on the tip of my pinkie like a tether tied from its heart to mine. It breathes as I breathe; it lives as I live. It will only close with a splash of my blood smeared through all the lines of paint, disrupting the magic.

"It's done," I tell Hadrian through the door, and he opens it. He studies me, assessing my condition, and even still, he doesn't look at the circle, for all that the runes on the floor shine like starlight.

"You should sleep," he says, slipping his hand across my back and guiding me down the hall, locking the door to the weaving room behind us. We take the key, which the staff had left on the top edge of the door frame, but I know they could pry their way in if they wanted to. For a moment, I consider leaving Hadrian to guard it, but he hears the thought before it forms in my throat. "I'll stay here, if you want. But you don't know what might be waiting for us in the mines."

I consider this. There might be monsters prowling the base of the mountain; there might not. I might need him; I might not. But the secrets of the teleportation circle are the most pivotal part of my trade as a phantom keeper.

In the end, I decide I'd rather live—I'd rather have him with me. Which means he also needs to sleep.

There's no easy way to clean the rune paint from my fingers, but the spell I just cast slowly uses up the excess, burning it away like candle wax. I wash my hands afterwards, relishing in the warmth of the water that Hadrian heats with a brush of his thumb. The way he casts is so subtle, I almost always miss the glimmer that flares along his skin, the hush of his breath, the pulse of effort that leaves his body. Without an open flame, it's the kind of magic that leaves no trace.

I eat, but I can't sleep. I try, but I lie awake for hours instead, counting the minutes, keeping my eyes closed in the hopes my body can be tricked into resting. Hadrian lies in a bed across the room, the frame just an inch too short for his legs, his knees bent, his arms tucked beneath his head. This guest room is just four doors down the hall from the room with my circle, and all night I wait to hear if a member of the staff will try the door, break the lock.

In the morning, I pretend to wake when Hadrian takes my hand, blinking my eyes owlishly, gawking at the window. But he isn't fooled even for a moment.

On the ride to the mines, the city is still, and there's no man at the eastern gate to let us through. It's like the people here are all holding their breath, waiting for peace, hoping for some resolution they can do nothing to bring about. Either I will manage what they've asked, or I will not.

AMANDA FERREIRA

Hadrian insists we take one horse, and on the short trek through the woods, the path well marked but deserted, I understand why. I'm asleep in moments at his back, my arms held loosely around his waist. How he managed to keep me in place with just a hand on my wrist I'll never know.

When I wake, I find we're alone at the base of the mountain, as alone as we'd been on the road. It's a small range, really more a collection of large hills, the mountains only growing in the far distance to the towering heights worthy of stories. There's no smell here, not even of pine trees or grass, and it's quiet, perfectly so, like the greyness of the stone used to build everything in Frostborro has bled into the very air here. It's ubiquitous, ominous.

Hadrian dismounts first. "Let me look."

It's a foolish thing to offer; if a monster lies in wait, I'd want us to face it together. But still, he insists, and I watch him go.

Sometimes, I forget Hadrian grew up in the wilderness; that he's more than a dutiful student or inquisitive astronomer. He's a natural-born tracker, a predator, and he moves with the grace of his birthright. He's quick on his feet, surveying the ground with long, loping strides, but he's tense, always ready to fight.

I can't remain on our horse. I feel useless, so I tie her to a stabling post, the wood cracked, the nearby water trough only half full of rain. She bends her neck but won't drink.

Uneasy, I reach behind me to string my bow. Hadrian didn't ask why I brought it here, when I have him to defend me; after all, it can't help with any spell, and it won't comfort the dead. Still, I never go anywhere without it.

I keep my gloves on, forcing a layer between me and the wood. Regardless, the power within hums in my hands, and

I taste a burning, vicious hunger in the back of my throat that doesn't belong to me.

I spit into the grass, trying to dislodge the bitterness, but realize suddenly that I've lost sight of Hadrian. That shouldn't be possible; the path in front of the mines is completely clear. The entrance is marked by a fallen sign, the rocks beyond moved only partially out of the way, creating the tiniest of openings. He wouldn't have gone in without me. He—

I start running. "Hadrian?"

He answers immediately from somewhere up ahead.

I creep into the edge of the woods where the trees grow right up against the foot of the mountain. From here, I can still see our horse, the entrance to the mines, and the sky. But when I step around a fallen tree, all those things shift out of focus.

There's a strong, overwhelming smell of rotting bodies here. And for good reason; there are dozens of overturned graves between the tree roots, and hunched over them is a monstrous thing, grotesque, with long arms and dirty, translucent skin. It's twice the size of me, doubled over, crunching on a bone. Blood is splattered all over its hands, which are hardly more than long, spidery fingers, picking, picking, picking at dead skin.

Hadrian is crouched on the ground behind a tree, hiding in the dense underbrush, watching it wearily.

Monsters of this kind have no name; they are numerous, coming in all shapes and sizes, but most are harmless and often no more intelligent than animals. Even this thing, with its back to the mountain and its feet in an open grave, is little more than a scavenger, opportunistic and spiteful. Still, when I put the pieces together and realize it's been gorging itself on the bodies of the dead miners, the stagnant wind keeping the smell and the sounds from bleeding out onto the road, I feel sick.

"What do we do?" I whisper, already forming a plan of attack in my mind. We don't have time for this—I don't have time for this—but surely an arrow or two could end this quickly.

Hadrian won't meet my eye. In his pride, they don't burn their dead; they bury them. It's why his kind of magic, manifesting at random, forced him to study at the academy; why his pride demanded perfect control and hired oversight. This is a horror that wounds him personally.

"Stay here," he says, and before I can stop him, he shifts.

Over all the years we've spent together, I've only seen this a handful of times, but always, the violence of the transformation surprises me. Hadrian yells, loud and pained, as every bone in his body splits apart, his jaw breaking in three places, his knees snapping backwards, his spine cracking in two. He grows and grows, fur, cartilage, and claws bursting from his body, a mane the colour of his hair circling his head. He's large enough to swallow our horse; large enough to barrel through the side of a house. His teeth are each the length of my hand, and his tail is like a whip, every movement stripping branches off trees. He's more than a lion; he's a force of nature.

He charges, head down, at this creature in its throng of bodies.

It howls, high and piercing, pieces of flesh and drops of blood slipping from its mouth. Its neck is long, too long for a body with such a humanoid head. It slashes carelessly at Hadrian, scoring his face.

I know I should let this play out; Hadrian, in his shifted form, is in little danger. His claws alone tear through the creature with relative ease, but—

22

As one of the monster's arms drops into the soil, twisting and bucking with the fading ends of nerves and life, two more burst from the same spot on its body. One head becomes two, mangled skin growing and regrowing from any place black blood blooms from an injury.

In an instant, it becomes a mound of limbs, of screams, of howls. It grows bigger, bigger than Hadrian, bigger than anything I've ever seen.

I have no spells to combat something like this. But I have my bow.

I pull off both gloves. I take the weapon in my hands, standing back in the undergrowth, nocking an arrow.

A man appears at my side, holding the bow between my upraised arms, his body translucent but material. A ghost; a phantom; my prisoner.

Aim true, he says in my head, like to do anything else would disappoint him, disgust him. I nod, and he disappears.

I'm a terrible shot without him to guide me, but my target is impossible to miss. The monster's fallen over, crippled by the weight of its own distorted body, a dozen heads screaming, two dozen legs clawing at the dirt.

I aim at its chest. I yell for Hadrian to stay out of the way.

I fire.

The air around the arrow crystallizes into a form only I can see. The man from before has transformed into a crow, monstrous and black, more wicked than poisoned blood, than death. This is the true power I possess, the true potential only I control.

He told me his name once, in a language he said I would understand. Elias. If I could aim at the moon, he swore he'd devour it.

His cry is a sharp thing, his talons like nets—nothing escapes. He cuts through the monster like its body is made of paper, cleaving it entirely in two. And as it struggles, it smokes, a magic beyond any that exists today dissolving it into paste.

The crow vandalizes what remains of its body, thrashing in the carnage, cawing, screeching.

I look at Hadrian in his lion form, wounded and bleeding, and wonder what he sees. I always do. Elias is a kind of phantom, the spirit of a shifter long dead, but he isn't visible to anyone but me. As long as I hold the bow against my bare skin, he breathes, his power entirely his own. Hadrian can see the monster's body falling apart, the sparks of magic breaking open its sodden, malformed flesh. But he can see no crow, no fallen god, no cost.

Elias, I think at him, knowing the battle is done. I tighten my grip on the bow, twisting the wood in my hands. *That's enough.*

The crow looks back at me. Elias says, *You know what you owe.*

I do. Our alliance is one I mostly beg for, but he knows I have my uses. Without me, he can't feed. Without me, he'd still be trapped in obscurity, lost on this plane.

I nod.

In an instant, Elias is gone. The monster drops, twitching in the bloody dirt. There's little of it left.

For all the magic that had been on display, I feel nothing. Unlike spells I cast myself, there's no personal cost to what Elias expends. But I collapse out of habit, gasping with practised ease, knowing what Hadrian will expect to see. I cast the spell on my right hand, the draw on my body bringing tears to my eyes.

When Hadrian shifts back to his human form, a moment of transformation I miss, he kneels next to me in the grass, holding me through the pain. He sees me winded, the rune paint under my clothes glowing like firelight. But in truth, none of that is real; I've cast nothing beyond a simple spell for a simple disguise. There's no need for anything else.

But, as part of the lie, I make myself shiver in his grasp, pretending to feel weak, almost faint. He pivots to squeezing my hand, trying to be soothing.

Once I've caught my breath, he presses his nose into my hair, affectionate in that shifter way of his. He doesn't know such a feat of destructive magic should've killed me, but Elias is from a different time, and as long as I keep him fed— as long as he eats, consumes, devours—his power is mine to weaponize.

He's a monster trapped in my bow, in a cage of my own making, imprisoned on this plane and in this place, tethered to me for as long as I live. He's the reason every other phantom keeper is dead. Their lives, their deaths—they were the first cost for his magic I ever paid. I was just an apprentice back then, but Elias made me worthy of more. Of fighting gods.

Godkiller. That's the closest translation to his true name —to the truest extent of his power. And as long as I have this bow, it is *mine*.

Dimly, I'm aware that Hadrian is trembling, that his breathing is awkward and strained. I pull back, and gradually, my skin stops glowing in the morning light.

I take him in, my gaze moving from one gash on his face to the next. He's bleeding profusely from his forehead, but he won't take his eyes from mine.

I push back his hair. "You're hurt."

He acts surprised. "I heal quickly. Though I don't know why I bothered getting involved. You had that."

I did; I could have ended the fight before it began. Instead, I point out, "We didn't know what it could do."

Hadrian nods, blood dripping down between his eyes. I wipe it away with my sleeve, pressing the fabric to the cuts on his face one by one. I realize, only then, that he's naked, all his clothes shredded from the shift to his lion form. I remove my robes.

"It'll have to do," he says, allowing me to drape it over his shoulders. He is, as always, without shame. I try not to look down. "Thank you for stepping in."

"You would have killed it," I tell him, though it's likely a lie. "You fought to honour the dead."

He turns to glance at what remains of the bodies in the clearing, at the monster still decaying before our eyes, the wind taking its brittle, broken bones between the trees like seedlings blown from a dandelion. Truly, Elias's power is unmatched, ungodly. "I tried," he acknowledges. "I tried."

CHAPTER FOUR

I remove the bindings on my arms and legs so I can dress Hadrian's wounds, the most severe already starting to form scabs. He hisses at the pressure but lets me work, his eyes tracking me as I go. I bind his calves, his shoulders, his throat, then help him redress, though my robes fit him poorly in the chest.

I want to wrap some of the linen around his forehead, but he refuses. Instead, he presses down on the gash whenever it begins to bleed again, as much to keep the blood out of his eyes as to aid in the healing.

"You can appreciate a man with scars, can't you?" he asks, his tone light and teasing. He's covered in scars, some faint and pink, some so small I've only ever noticed them when we're like this, his skin in my hands, his new injuries exposed.

"Many women do," is my answer. He tilts his head, breathing me in.

Even without shoes, Hadrian insists on walking in front of me back towards the mines, his stride hardly seeming to slow over twigs, stones, or uneven earth. We've reburied what we can of the gravesite, but without tools, our work is haphazard; we'll have to raise it with the mayor when we return to the city.

At the entryway into the mountain, Hadrian sticks his entire torso into the hole the surviving miners had managed to dig out of the collapsed tunnel. "It widens just past here," he says, pulling himself out and gesturing to it, loose dirt falling out of his hair. "How far in do you want to go?"

From here, I can't sense any of the dead. "As far as I need to," I say cryptically, for there's no real way to gauge the distance. "I won't know until I find them."

Hadrian nods, allowing me to crawl through the gap first, emerging into what remains of a space lined with mining carts partially crushed by rubble. Wooden support beams and broken metal lanterns lay strewn in the rocks and dirt, but some are still attached to the ceiling, holding the mountain at bay. I press my palm to the stone, willing the gods to keep things steady and still a little while longer.

"Maybe you should stay out there," I shout back through the gap in the rocks. "If the rest of the tunnel collapses, we both don't have to die."

The words hang heavy in the air.

Of course, Hadrian pushes himself through the tiny hole without responding, emerging even more tattered, somehow, in the half-light. He raises one of his hands, and with a snap of his fingers, a small blue flame bursts to life on his palm. There's no smoke, and if I stepped closer to check, no heat. He motions the way forward.

I try to follow the voices of the dead, but it takes hours of wandering down dark, stuffy corridors to pick up even a faint whisper of them, so soft is their calling, so feeble their hope. I turn at the next branch of tunnels and find the way blocked. Most of the ways forward are blocked.

This is quickly turning into something impossible. "They're here," I say vaguely, and just the sound of my voice, hushed and gentle, unsettles the dirt. Hadrian coughs. "But I don't know if we'll be able to get close enough."

"Two more turns," he suggests, loosening where I've tied my robes closed at his throat. Without the knots, he's exposed where I pulled bandages across his shoulders and neck, most of the red stains already dark. "There were survivors. There must be some way that leads on."

Four turns later, and at last we find all possible ways forward have caved in. I can hear the whispering a little louder now, coming from straight ahead. Cautiously, I pick up a rock slightly larger than my hand from the middle of the collapsed wall, expecting to see packed dirt on the other side, but there's nothing, only darkness. Hadrian sticks his arm through the hole.

It takes some digging, but we manage to unearth the entrance into a cavernous room, the high ceiling towering over us. When I run my hands over the glittering dots of pale white light lining the walls, I find they aren't gems, exactly, but veins of something cold, semi-precious. If ground into powder, I suspect it could mix into paints or blush. If cored out, it might sell to a city far south of here, where the mountains hold nothing but aged, weathered stone.

I sit in the center of the space, beginning to hum in time with the calling. Hadrian sits with his back against mine, the light in his hand blazing brighter, the warmth of his body a balm.

I'm close enough to sense them now, and I can feel it, the faint flickering of each life trapped on this plane. Words drift out of the dust and the rocks as the ghosts swirl around me, searching, aching. *Is it over? Is it you?*

Hadrian can't hear the voices. From where he sits, we're all alone in the quiet, the mountain dead or dying, the walls still, waiting for nothing. And it's dark, horribly dark, even with the light of his flame. He sneezes twice, rubbing his nose on the sleeve of my robes, but he doesn't speak.

I can almost feel the ghosts as they brush past my cheeks, twirling around my arms and across my face. I can't see them yet, in this form, but they sound thankful, relieved, that I'm here, that I've come. Ghosts can't cry, but they can remember the feeling of sadness, of pain.

I hold out my hands. I don't have to do this—it does nothing for them or for me—but I like the monotony of it, of tracing the runes I've painstakingly painted all over my body. They're cold, and the paint is stiff, the tiny hairs on my arms plastered to my skin.

I don't need to expose the runes for this to work; the magic draws from me regardless. But still, I love to see it. I love to see the moment magic remakes who I am.

The white rune paint glows faintly silver as I begin. It feels so much like drawing in a breath that sometimes I miss when the spell first takes hold. Then, slowly, the silver turns gold as the runes burn away, the paint flaking into dust.

I've painted enough of my body to give colour to a hundred ghosts, a thousand. The spell is the same either way, but the demand on my body spikes sharply with the needs of each ghost.

All around me, all at once, they burst into ribbons of coloured light as they swirl along the walls of the room. I can tell that they're scared, but they're trusting. They always are.

As I reveal them, they become anchored to me, and they

can sense the invisible tether tied to my pinky; they know, perhaps instinctually, that it will lead them back to the teleportation circle I've drawn in the mayor's estate. They can sense it *through* me, my body acting as a conduit, a guide.

Hadrian doesn't turn. He doesn't look. If he did, he would see so many of my secrets laid bare across my skin. But he never does. I decide, in that moment, that he is a wonder.

From the pouch at my waist, I discretely pull out two small glass vials and cradle them both in one hand. The other hand I hold aloft, the magic emanating off my arm like a lighthouse, the power slowly pulling more phantoms—no longer ghosts, once in colour—towards me. Exhaustion sets in around the edges of my mouth and the corners of my eyes as I burn another spell from a rune traced along my hip, the pain sharp.

I choose two of the balls of light at random, dipping the vials into them like I might capture a spoonful of mist. They slip inside, unknowing, unable to resist. I cork the vials carefully, sealing them airtight.

When I get to my feet, the vials are hidden back in my pouch, each wrapped in silk so the glass won't knock together, giving away what I've done. Hadrian will never know, and neither will the townsfolk. What are just two souls among a hundred?

The other phantoms brush against my hands in gratitude. They are palpable, if only just; they can tease the air and rustle my clothes but can do no harm. Hadrian watches for these movements, for any evidence the phantoms are there, but rarely sees any. This time, the trail of just one manages to catch his eye.

A brilliant blue phantom tucks itself behind my ear, pulling at my jaw, then wraps back around to pass through my hair. Hadrian follows the path with his finger. The phantom then drifts through the hole we've dug in the entrance to this room and disappears down the tunnel, drawn to my teleportation circle far in the distance.

Hadrian lowers his hand just a little, his fingers still in my hair. I remind myself that the closeness isn't unusual for him; that among his pride, his people, casual touch even in human form is common.

But this...feels intimate. Perhaps it's the fire burning in his other hand, casting his face in a pale blue glow, the shadows across his nose catching on the angles of his face, his cheeks, his lips. Perhaps it's the darkness beyond his pool of light, the quiet, the thickness of the air. Perhaps it's the feeling that we're standing in the center of the earth, above the beating heart of this mountain, of the world.

He could kiss me, if he wanted to. He could lean in so quickly, so easily, and then the moment would be ours. I let myself imagine it, even crave it.

But he only looks at me, and I look back. He drops his hand. "You saw it," he says softly. "Was I right?"

The path of the phantom, I assume. "You were," I whisper back.

He smiles, then tilts his head. "You're shaking."

I am. And I can't tell if it's from the demands of the spell or the closeness of him. His eyes are so bright in the darkness that they're all I can focus on.

I blink, swallow, then turn away.

I remind myself there are things I'm not allowed to want.

Together, we make our way back out of the tunnels. "Go," I murmur over my shoulder time and again, and always, another phantom appears from behind a rock, behind a support beam, as if waiting for me. "You know the way."

Some are laughing. Some are singing. They are sweet and joyous and willful again. I find the energy in my heart to envy them, though I'm so afraid to die.

Emerging into the daylight, I watch as all the remaining trails of colour drift away. I'll feel very little as each phantom passes over the circle, sneaking into the room full of looms through the window I've left ajar, but I always know when the last one is gone. It's just a feeling, like many others, that I will never be able to explain.

I make it a handful of steps farther before staggering, the cost of the magic cutting me off at the knees. I drop to the ground, my head drooping down on my chest. There's no need to fake the bile that rises in my throat this time, and I spit into the dirt.

Hadrian has to carry me to our horse, and he rides with me in his lap, my body limp in his arms. The last thing I see, before falling asleep, is the curve of his shoulder and the bright, golden gleam of the sun.

CHAPTER FIVE

I don't know how much time passes, but I remember little of the afternoon. Hadrian must carry me to bed, though, because I wake up back in our borrowed room, his cloak draped over me like a second blanket, my head stacked two pillows high on goose down and silk sheets. The air is crisp, tasting of summer, and moves when a breeze drifts through the window, but it's rained since we left the mines. My clothes smell like I've been sitting out in the storm, watching for lightning, waiting for the clouds to break.

Hadrian sleeps in the bed next to mine, the frames pushed together, our bodies flush. In the fading amber light, the rich brown of his arms looks even darker, his skin tanned a deeper shade by the long hours we've spent in the sun. He's lying on his stomach, his face turned towards the wall, his shoulders still bundled beneath my shoddy excuse for bandages. I reach out to wake him, expecting to see a flash of his dazzling green eyes in the dark, but he doesn't stir.

As his snores continue, soft and unbroken, I slip from our conjoined bed. He needs his sleep, maybe more than I do; for all that his bones break and his skin tears and his body remakes itself when he shifts, he claims it isn't painful, just exhausting. *It's a little uncomfortable, but only for a moment, then it's over.*

I admire him; his ability to sleep so soundly just about anywhere is a skill I would pay to possess.

Leaving him to his dreams, I cross the room to glance out the window, drawn by the sound of people in the streets. Outside, the city is lively; there are lanterns lit atop high posts, coloured flags raised in the waterlogged wind, and singing heavy in the air. Perhaps they're celebrating our return; I'll never know. Perhaps they feel some sense of closure, even though there's no proof anything was done.

I remind myself that it shouldn't matter; that I shouldn't care what they think or what they know. If they want to celebrate based on nothing but blind faith, I should let them —proving I've done my work isn't technically part of the job. And what could I say, if they asked? I can't show them the circle, and by now, all the phantoms are gone.

At the end of the day, on jobs like these, getting paid —and taking my cut of the dead—is all that counts. After all, it's only the money, the fees, that keeps me from doing the menial labour other students at the academy are reduced to, like working the farms or tending the animals on the lower isles, grinding grain and picking fruit. For most, this is the only way to pay for their studies, the exorbitant cost of books and quills and tuition stacking up quickly.

But somewhere, perhaps in the furthest reaches of my consciousness, whether I can admit it or not, I *do* care, otherwise I wouldn't bother doing this the way I do. I could easily lie, claim I'd helped, and be on my way. Who would ever know the difference?

But where the order of keepers would stoop so low

when it served them—when they felt any particular request was beneath the use of rune paint—I refuse.

I have to be better than them. I will be. I am.

Pushing my hair back with my hand, I stand with my hip against the cold stone of the wall, idly tapping one of my fingers against the window, disturbing a few beads of rain on the other side. *I should be resting*, I reprimand myself. *We have a lot of riding ahead of us.* But I don't turn. The weight of the two vials in my pouch, of the two souls caged within, weigh on me.

In the coming weeks, before our return to the academy, I'll have to find the time to release them, to feed Elias. But with Hadrian and I growing as close as we have, opportunities to get away are few and far between.

It's a problem I'll have to solve another day.

I remind myself of my priorities, going over them like a mantra: build my name, keep my power. That's it. That's really all.

I'll find a way to lie to Hadrian. I'll put some space between us, if I have to.

But it's easier said than done.

When Hadrian turns onto his back in his bed, the sound drawing my eyes across the room, a flicker of something strange—almost painful—flashes through my mind. Hadrian's hair is mussed, his lips red, his injuries exposed, and seeing him forces me to remember that I've involved him in my schemes whether he's aware of it or not. And he's hurt right now, quite badly in some places, because of *me*. If I had come alone, there'd be no need to keep anything from him, and I wouldn't have thought to look in the woods. Perhaps I wouldn't have fought that creature at all.

But now he's complicit—at least a little—in most of my lies. For every soul I save, another is sacrificed, the blood price paid. For every creature I kill or target I strike, Elias must be appeased. Elias must always be fed.

Hadrian murmurs something when he wakes, sounding sleepy, his smile easy and warm. I hadn't realized how long I'd been standing at the window, how long I'd been listening to him breathe.

He calls out my name, that other name, searching for me. It's short and clipped, harsh and ill-fitting. It unsettles me, and I suddenly can't bring myself to respond to it.

He rolls over again, the wood beneath him creaking. His hair is tied back in a loose braid, the blond bright and stark against his skin. When he spots me, he says, "Come back to bed."

Then he says my name again, the name that isn't my name. It's too much.

In my reflection in the window, in the pale glimmer in the glass, I look at my face. My jaw is lean and slim, my nose sharp, my features hard. I had been softer, once, before Elias's skills demanded more of me, and now muscle has replaced the faint curves I'd come to love. Even my mouth is unforgiving, with thin lips and little in the way of arch or colour.

Maybe I'm delirious, when I choose what I'm about to say. Maybe I'm overtired and overstimulated, hyperfixating on a version of my life I'll never live. Maybe my guarded, icy, thorny heart has been moved, just a little, by the only friend I've allowed myself to have in over a decade. Two.

Or maybe I'm just tired of lying to him.

I face Hadrian head on. "Pella," I say aloud. Pea-la. I can't remember the last time I did such a thing. "Will you call me Pella?"

Hadrian leans up on his arms, and I notice all at once that he's been sleeping without a pillow; behind him, my bed has two. He's changed into another set of his clothes, donning a tight, dark shirt, open at the neck but without sleeves, so his arms and shoulders are on full display. In his human form, he's as determined and persistent as the animal he carries in his blood, prepared for anything. But perhaps not for this.

After a long moment of silence, he says, "Pella. It's a woman's name."

I don't want to argue with him; I know what it is. What I am. I can't remember how to move more than my eyes. I watch him a moment longer, waiting.

He considers this, then says it again. "Pella." His green eyes, verdant, shimmering, find mine in the darkness. "May I call you 'girl' as well?"

May I.

It unsettles me, his cool, neutral reaction. His request. Surely the gods wouldn't allow me to know such a person as this, who would accept me so openly, so easily.

Before this moment, before meeting this man, I've had to fight for everything I have, for everything I am. Everything I've left behind has been by my own design, cut off as abruptly and brutally as if by a sword swing, and everyone who once knew me is long dead. I prefer it that way.

Now, I am laid bare.

Returning to myself, I incline my head. "When we're alone." It's the only answer I can imagine offering.

Eventually, Hadrian nods.

We don't speak on it again until the morning, when I'm crouched knee-deep in enough soapy water to bathe in. The basin I've dragged into the weaving room is dark with blood and ruined rune paint, the floor scored by harsh brush strokes. I always aim to leave nothing of my work behind, if I can manage it.

My left hand stings. The soap is harsh and the cut on my palm is deep, the blood needed to break the teleportation circle no small thing. I've stitched my hand, tying off the wound with a sturdy thread, but I forgot to bring salve. The injury throbs as I work, my heartbeat pushing more blood to the surface of my skin.

"Would mine have worked?" Hadrian asks when he brings me another cup of tea. It's become a comfort, this routine, on trips like these. I stop to drink, and though my right hand is free, my left only holding a rag, he insists on holding the cup, bringing it carefully to my lips as I drink. "My blood, I mean."

Water runs down my forearm and drips onto the floor. The sound is rhythmic, almost musical. "It has to be mine," I tell him. "The circle is permanent otherwise."

He watches me drink, the large cup easy to spill if he's not careful. It's almost a flagon, really, meant for ale or beer. I imagine he's had to brew a few large piles of leaves to get the flavour this rich.

"Pella," he says eventually, over the sound of my sips. Pea-la. Oh, how the name cuts me deep, right down to the bone.

I find I can't face him, so I turn away. "Yes?"

Hadrian hesitates. Swallows. "How long have you known?"

If there were other people in my life, other people I trusted, perhaps this wouldn't be the first time someone's asked me this. But I don't, so it is. "A long time. Years, maybe."

I take the mostly full cup in my empty hand. Blood,

soap, and paint discolours the handle, but Hadrian lets it leave his grasp.

He says, "Tell me what to do."

"Don't do anything," I reply. "Don't do anything else differently. Not in front of anyone."

He steps into the room, if only to find and hold my gaze, serious and calm. "And in private?" he asks, his voice so low it seems to rumble out of his chest. "What then?"

I'm almost relieved he's still flirting with me. There's something harmless in it, something I've come to appreciate in the otherwise brash, upfront, no-nonsense way he approaches his life. *This* is as close to delicate as he comes.

I consider my answer. "Just...call me Pella. That's all I ask."

I return to the bucket and the brush and the pile of used, dirty rags, setting the tea to the side, away from where a bad splash would ruin the brew. My hand still aches, my bow is still cursed, and my pouch is still full of souls. But my heart feels lighter.

Hadrian helps me clean the rest of the floor.

CHAPTER SIX

On the ride to the headlands, to the cliffs that overlook the valleys and the hillsides of Vesperdeep, Hadrian is tense, hounded by an overwhelming sense of dread. "What if they're dead?" he says, and I can't comfort him; I don't know how. "What if the entire pride is gone?"

He worries about this until the forest gives way to open road, and the open road to endless plains. All of it is new to me; I've seen mountains, snow, and even the wild heart of a cloying, choking jungle, but not this—this rolling expanse, boundless and wide, is so vast it's like being lost at sea. I feel like I'm drowning in it.

We ride until the horses tire, then rest where the wind tastes almost faintly of wheat. "Is it always like this?" I ask him, and he laughs, his joy bright and infectious. It glows under his skin, making him look younger, almost boyish.

"Except when it rains," he says. "That's a wholly different kind of magic."

Seeing this place, I can better understand how Hadrian used to live—how he used to spend his days in shifted form, how he rarely took the time to study or write. Now, I can see the threat he truly posed out here, once he discovered his magic; how a wildfire could spread with no safeguards in sight. But for a soul like his, meant to be fearless and free, surely there's no worse fate than being caged on the isles forever, for all that it's a fate he could change, if he wanted to. I still don't know why he doesn't.

"Does it still feel like home?" I whisper, watching his eyes drink in the world like a man drunk on the wind.

Hadrian pats the neck of his horse, his other hand restless at his side. I wonder what he's thinking; what he misses most. "Nothing is different," he says, smiling to himself. Then he takes my hand and kisses my knuckles, his lips cool against my skin. The gratitude is so unexpected that I feel myself blush. "Thank you for bringing me here, for taking me with you."

"My pleasure," is what I say, though the words hardly form on my tongue. *Anything to see you this happy.*

Hours of riding later, once everything for our camp tonight is settled, Hadrian pulls his horse closer to the stream, tying her lead to a tree next to mine. We're nearly out of food, but share the dried meats and nuts that remain. He'd offered to hunt, but the stretch of grassland nearest us is empty and still. This will have to do.

Tucked in my bedroll, I sleep fitfully while Hadrian takes first watch, his attention on the plains as he scans for signs of bandits or roaming, monstrous things. I wake twice in the first hour, blurry-eyed and dazed, certain it's my turn to sit by our small fire. Each time, Hadrian smiles ruefully and gauges the passing minutes on his fingers.

Eventually, I do manage to stay asleep, but when Hadrian wakes me in truth, I find it's well past an equal split in the night.

"You needed it," he says, and I wave him off.

"If we see your family tomorrow, *you'll* need it," I reply.

His pained, hopeful smile is a thing of tragedy. We only have one more day to spend on the plains, and unless his pride comes upon us by chance, the odds are poor we'll cross their path. Still, any chance at all is more than we'd had before, and Hadrian accepts it with greed.

I wait for him to fall asleep in the grass, for his breathing to soften and his body to relax. Then I prod his shoulder. I prepare a quick lie, but he doesn't stir. He sleeps soundly.

Putting out the last embers of the fire, hoping the shadows will hide Hadrian for the short time I'll be gone, I draw my bow from its case and tie on the string, taking only a few arrows from my quiver as I set out. I tell myself that I won't need more. I promise myself that if I do, I'll forgo this whole attempt halfway.

There was little cover in which to set up camp, but as I leave our tiny dip in the hillside, the nearest clearing feels altogether too exposed. So I jog beneath the moonlight, my bow in one hand and the arrows in the other, until I'm overcome with a sudden sense of desperation that knocks the air from my chest.

I stumble, then land so hard in the grass I'm sure I've bruised both my knees. Elias is yelling.

His human form is always startling to see, his limbs long and limber, his scowl deep. His eyes and mine are the same dark green, his skin just as pale, his hair just as short. Sometimes, I think he's taken this form just to frighten me, to resemble me as much as he can. How else could it be possible that we look so similar?

Dazed, I tighten my grip on my bow, watching Elias pace in my field of sight. He can touch me, grab me, hurt me, if he wants to try.

He does.

43

With his fingers around my neck, Elias pushes me head-first into the grass, and for a moment, I think he means to smother me. He has enough power, like this, to kill me. But why? And why now?

I struggle against his hold just as something cuts into my back. Something silent and quick.

I roll to the left and watch as a shadow—a monster, dark and slim—pulls back into the air. I barely catch sight of it, of a carapace splattered with blood, of a segmented body framed by pincers and too many wings. It's the same colour as the sky, a dark and musty umber, so it's only when it passes in front of a cluster of stars that I realize the sheer horror of its size.

I'd only come here to release one of the two souls I'd trapped, to give Elias something to eat. I'd only needed ten minutes of solitude. This was supposed to be simple.

Elias can't touch anything in his human form besides me, and if I let go of the bow, he'll disappear. So he's no defence against this creature—worse than no defence at all.

And I only have four arrows with me. I only have four shots.

The monster makes no sound. Elias stands between it and me, knowing if I die, he dies.

He could shoot it. With his hands on my hands, both our fingers on the bow, he can hit anything, living or dead, a target of any size at any distance. But four arrows can't kill a beast that large.

In his shifted form, he can strike what the arrow strikes, but I know I'll miss it without his help, and only his human form can guide my hands.

For all my power, *his* power, I'm not infallible.

My back has been sliced into four ribbons, and I can

feel a surge of panic dulling the pain. Even still, it hurts to move; it hurts to breathe.

If I do nothing, I'll die.

So I run.

There are only a few lines of rune paint left on my body —a single defensive spell on my left hand. I have nothing else saved, nothing else spared, and I'm still so, so tired.

The creature dives, and I can just barely hear it; its pincers whistle by my ear, drawing more blood.

When it dives again, I cast the shield spell, hitting the dirt to avoid being crushed by the weight of its body, jarring my teeth. Elias is yelling again in a language I don't understand, his voice filling my head.

I remember screaming. And then my vision bursts with harsh, red light.

The heat of an open flame sears past me, the inferno barrelling over my head and into the sky. It strikes nothing, but it's impossibly loud; it burns and cracks and sparks and booms like thunder breaking over the side of a mountain.

Hadrian stands over me, his body ablaze. His arms are wrapped in fire, the red turning orange, then yellow, then white. It's so hot my skin starts to blister, and I have to shield my face. I immediately lose sensation in my hands.

He hurls another fireball into the sky, and this one catches that thing, that creature. It shrieks and cries and incinerates, its voice consumed by the blaze.

Its body crashes into the earth like a house exploding, its flesh burning and burning and burning. It is molten; it is melting. It sets all the surrounding grass on fire in a flash of colour.

The flames are everywhere, stretching as far as I can see in any direction. The monster dies in a mass of snapping, bubbling flesh, but Hadrian waits to be sure it's dead. Then he snaps his fingers and all the fire goes out.

I realize, in the darkness, that I'm crying. I'm alive, but my arms hurt so much I can hardly think past the agony of it.

Hadrian turns, glancing down, and the look on his face staggers me. He can't feel the heat of his own fire magic; he can't have known.

"Pella." He's yelling now, I think, but I can't hear him clearly over the sound of my own screams. My throat is raw, but my arms—even just the air hitting my skin is too much. It's too much.

I can't remember how to be afraid. I can't remember if I dropped my bow or if it had turned to ash in my ruined hands.

I force myself to close my eyes. There's a shooting pain in the back of my head, a ringing that's getting louder and louder and louder.

I want to die. I wish I was dead.

I let go.

CHAPTER SEVEN

There's something bitter in my mouth when I wake. A leaf, perhaps. Some kind of salve.

I can't open my eyes. Or, rather, when I do, I see nothing but shadows.

Slowly, an awareness of my body comes back to me: an ache in my shoulders, a numbness in both my arms. My hands are tied together at the wrist, but the bindings are soft, the knots loose. I could pull myself free if I wanted to, but I can't summon the energy to move.

Gradually, I piece together that I'm lying on my back, my arms above my head, my eyes covered, my body tucked beneath something warm. There's the smell of something cooking, the sound of a twinkling stream, the dampness of something on my brow. The world beyond me is still as I remember it, even if I can't see it.

I count backwards from ten, hoping to calm myself, but when I open my mouth, the mush coating my teeth becomes odd and sticky. I find it impossible to talk. I try to swallow, but I can't manage that either. I start choking.

Immediately, there's a presence at my side, and the

sound of someone dropping into the dirt. Their intention is kind, their fingers gentle on my skin, their touch so known to me that I recognize it blind. Hadrian slides his arms under my back, turning my body, and I'm able to spit over my shoulder until the mixture is gone. "I'm sorry," Hadrian says. "It's for the pain. It's supposed to help."

I don't know what to think, so I try not to think at all. I feel like a fever has left me stricken for weeks. The dampness on my face has disappeared, likely the wet cloth falling from my brow. Hadrian replaces it as he eases me down again, centering my head beneath my bound arms.

We don't speak for a long time. I'm almost not sure I can.

Eventually, Hadrian says, "We're safe now."

I swallow dryly. "Are we?" I manage to murmur, my voice scratchy and rough. I can't decide what to prioritize— what would be worse for the fire to have burned away. If I've lost my bow, I am nothing. If I've lost my hands, I am nothing. If I've lost both, I'd rather be dead.

Hadrian kisses my cheek. It's the most intimate form of apology he could choose. I shudder at the touch.

I don't want the answer, but I have to ask. "Is it bad?" My voice breaks. "Hadrian, please."

He sighs.

I assume the warmth over my body is my bedroll, but now I imagine my blanket is a white sheet, my skin charred and unrecognizable. I feel like I've been covered with a funeral shroud.

Hadrian removes my blindfold.

As my eyes focus, I'm struck by his expression—I've never seen such sorrow on his face before. Hadrian is beautiful when he smiles, so this is like looking at his body without a soul in it. He's clearly embarrassed, maybe even ashamed. And worse, he looks guilty; profoundly so.

I raise my eyes. My arms are wrapped in green leaves from elbow to wrist, my hands covered in what looks like seaweed. I can feel almost nothing of them. Beyond that, Hadrian has anchored my wrists to one of our packs, keeping my arms from lying in the hard-packed dirt.

I pull on the ties. The restraints break, and I'm able to move my arms in front of me. My left hand, my non-dominant hand, has fared better than my right; I can curl my fingers a little, and still use my thumb. My right hand feels like it's not even attached to my body anymore.

When I remove all the wrappings I can, my skin is red and uneven. Bloody. Parts are peeling, parts have blistered, and my veins look like they've been shot through with tar.

I can't imagine trying to write. Not like this.

"How long?" I ask him next. How many more answers will I survive? "How long do we have to get back?"

"You've only been out for two days," he whispers. "We have time."

I lower my hands to my sides. The moment they touch the ground, every inch of them throbs, and I immediately see the wisdom in Hadrian's decision to keep them aloft. But I can't bear to look at them, to see the damage. A building pressure thrums in my ears like a heartbeat. Even if my bow survived, could I draw back the string?

I decide to look for it, but I don't have to look for long. The moment I glance around our makeshift camp, Hadrian turns behind him and holds the bow before me, the wood in one—perfect—unblemished piece. Even the string is still intact, though the bow itself is unstrung. He's cared for it, my Hadrian.

The relief that overwhelms me is a powerful thing,

expansive and glorious, so palpable I can feel it in my throat and between my ribs. It's bright and wondrous and dazzling and sweet, and I try not to cry at the taste of it.

I know I should thank Hadrian for saving my life, but I need time to process what can be done, what else can be salvaged.

Suddenly, he says, "I understand if you can't forgive me. You've been in so much pain, and I—I'm so sorry."

I look at him then, really look at him. He's made himself small at my bedside, his head hanging low, his ears red, his eyes glassy. He's suffered too, in his own way. He's tended to me with all the supplies we have, with all the skills and remedies he knows.

I want to be hateful. Bitter. Frustrated. But to what end? I know Hadrian would never hurt me—not on purpose. How I feel about him is still the same.

I think to say, "Is there something to forgive?"

In his surprise, Hadrian chokes out a laugh. It's somber and forced, but it eases something inside me, some tension I hadn't realized was there.

He won't look at me. He breathes through his nose, and though his body relaxes, his fleeting expression of shock doesn't fade.

I wish I knew what to say, but all that comes to me are the words I know I believe. "What happened isn't your fault."

Again, I'm met with silence. Hadrian shifts on his knees, readjusting his weight, still avoiding my eyes. I know I must be drugged, my pain stifled, but I can still think clearly. I tell myself I can.

"We'll see how the burns look in a few weeks," I whisper. I don't know where this compassion is coming from; it doesn't feel like it belongs to me. "Until then, don't—"

"Blame myself?" he offers. "Pella, I could've killed you."

I close my eyes. "You saved my life," I remind him. Perhaps he's ruined it as well, but there's no way to know just yet. And if he hasn't, then I'm alive because of him. *Elias* is alive because of him. "And I'm grateful for that."

Finally—*finally*—Hadrian seems to relent. He leans forward, pressing his forehead against my chest, then moves the rest of his body closer until he's curled at my side.

I move slowly in answer, my arms finding their way around his neck. I've never embraced him before, and for all that it hurts, it feels right. I'm angry, but not at him; not really.

We stay like that for a long time, his breathing uneven, the fire burning out. Then he buries his face in the crook of my neck, careful not to jostle my arms. And though he doesn't speak again, he lets me hold him while he cries, and I promise him I won't let him go.

CHAPTER EIGHT

Hadrian guides my horse on a lead for the first three days of the ride back to the academy. By the fourth, my back and my thighs hurt so much from the tension needed to stay perfectly upright that I nearly fall out of the saddle.

By some miracle, Hadrian dismounts quickly enough to catch me, my body listing to the side, one stirrup lost, the other tangled around my boot. Everything hurts, and I want to lie down almost as much as I don't want to die.

Hadrian helps me sit on an overturned log facing the road. "We have time," is all he'll say. But I can feel the world growing darker by the day, almost like sand shifting ominously in an hourglass. If we ride any slower, I'm sure we'll miss the ship meant for our return. But if we ride any faster, all the jostling will break what remains of my spirit.

Carefully, Hadrian removes the bandages from my arms and hands, the poultice he's mixed smelling of rain, pine needles, and periwinkle. There are a few other things he's added that I can't name, the colours and textures all mashed together. He offers me a spoonful to chew, but I refuse.

"What is it?" I ask, shivering as he slathers it generously

on my injuries. I can't watch him while he works; can't look at the destruction of my skin. As it is, I shake profusely under his hands, and my eyes water as the mixture sets, rogue tears spilling down my nose.

I don't want Hadrian to see me cry, so I'm quick to turn my head towards the woods, watching over our shoulders for some threat between the trees. I remember to breathe in through my nose and out through my mouth, so slowly my chest hardly moves at all.

It burns. Everything burns. I feel as tender as a newborn babe, sensitive to light and sound and wind and any roughness at all. I can barely move any of the fingers on my right hand, though some amount of feeling has started coming back in my palm. I pray the numbness is because of the blisters, because of the agony of my split skin, and nothing more.

"It's a family concoction," Hadrian eventually says, and he's even gentler now, working the salve between each of my knuckles and down the backs of my hands. "I...set a good number of things on fire when my magic first presented."

I nod, trying to swallow down a sudden wave of hysteria as a sharp pain flares around my wrists. At some point, what seems like a lifetime later, it dissipates. Hadrian squeezes my knee. "Do you regret going to the academy for help?" I ask him.

I can't see his face, but I can hear how his voice tightens. "Almost every day," he says. "They're cowards. No one would agree to go if they knew the cost."

When I turn back to him, his expression is hard. "You could leave," I remind him. "We're only a few days' ride from your home. You could stay."

"Oh?" he says lowly, though it's a fact he and I both know. "And what of you?"

His vibrant, piercing, all-knowing green eyes drop to my hands. I dare to look, but can only see the delicate way he's wrapped them, flower stems and petals tucked between the folds of leaves and cloth. It smells like a garden now, like herbs and spices, mint and clove. I realize, all at once, that all the extra work is meant to mask the scent of burnt flesh.

His thoughtfulness winds me.

"I want to go back," I say bluntly, and it's more a reminder for me than an answer for him. The headmaster has seen my potential; she's seen what Elias can do, even if she wrongly ascribes his power to my hand. Royal courts have sent me to kill monsters in their mountains, assassinate rivals in their beds. I've seen every side of opulence, been offered rooms full of gold, been treated to the finest foods imaginable. I know I can't be more than a few steps away from my ultimate goal.

There's no higher seat of power than the council that controls the Academy of Light. They puppet kings, over-turn laws, drown cities, twist history. And now that I'm noteworthy enough, I've aspired to join them—I've worked hard to earn the faith and the trust needed to catch their eye. And once I'm on the council, everything will change. The *world* will change. Every royal family on the continent owes me a favour. All the other phantom keepers are dead.

All the other phantom keepers are dead.

Hadrian brushes something off my face, and I realize he's still waiting for the rest of my response. "There's so much I want to do," I tell him truthfully. "So much more I want to learn."

Hadrian tilts his head, reaching forward to pull me up

by my shoulders. His hands are hot, so hot they leave impressions through my clothes. I can feel the ghost of each of his fingers on my body, against my skin.

I'm nearly there, I want to argue. I have a name that the kingdom knows, a reputation that precedes me, a kind of magic so rare that it's otherwise gone.

"Pella," Hadrian says. "When was the last time they taught you something useful? If anything, they should be learning from *you*."

The thought makes me smile. "That's true," I admit. But there's no time to debate this, and I'm not sure I want to.

Drawing back to my horse, I gesture to the saddle. "Will you give me a boost?" My muscles ache, but my resolve is solid, unflinching.

Hadrian takes my elbow, his touch light and careful. "Ride with me," he says. "It will be easier."

When we finally bed down for the night, paying for a room at the first inn with room for two, I'm in so much pain I can hardly move. Even thinking is difficult. And bathing is a whole other matter.

It takes only a moment to realize I can't undress myself. With what limited grip I have in my left hand, I can't even loosen a knot without mind-numbing, excruciating pain.

So I'm left to feel useless, incompetent, in a tiny, claustrophobic room, next to a string of shiny metal tubs lined up against the wall. I can't even bring myself to ask Hadrian for help—he's already offered, and I've already refused. Now, he just watches me idly, the water in the room growing cold. I'm trying not to struggle. I'm stuck halfway out of my shirt.

"Do you think the innkeeper would care if I bathed with all my clothes on?" I ask him, and in response, he huffs, then pulls himself out of his tub.

Hadrian is gentle, where he touches me. I let him help. I have no other choice.

When he gets to the layer of bandages covering my back, he grimaces. I catch his reflection on the edge of the nearest copper tub. "Is it bad?"

He steps aside, giving me the space to turn and regard the injury. "It looks like someone tried to rip you in two," he says. "The cuts run high, between your shoulders."

It's true. But the wounds are shallow, the outer slashes thinner than the center ones. They might heal; they might fade.

"I'm sorry," I murmur, raising my eyes to take in the ceiling, to study the width of the wood grain and the peeling edges of the varnish and dark paint. "I feel like a child who can do nothing for themselves. And things will only get worse from here."

I shudder at the thought, at trying to imagine writing my essays, compiling my notes, mixing my potions, painting my spells.

Hadrian chooses to disregard my embarrassment and ignore my shame. "Anything you need of me," he says softly, "you need only ask. Now, and when we return to the academy. However I can help, I will. You have my word."

"There's no debt between us," I tell him, just as he reaches for the knot at the front of my trousers, easing his fingers through the loop. He raises his eyes when they fall. "I won't allow it."

He waits for me to submerge in the nearest tub, then returns to his own. The water is cool, blessedly so; it eases the pain, if only for a moment.

I tell myself I *will* recover from this. I have to. Otherwise, without my spells, my runes, my bow, my *power*, what else do I have?

The thought is loud. Sobering. I chew on it, all while trying not to look at my hands.

CHAPTER NINE

It takes several months after our return to the academy—time that passes in a blur of salves, stretches, bandages, and healing—for the letters from Frostborro to reach me. The bundle of eight is wrapped in string, each wax seal broken, each corner torn, just like all the mail we receive here.

"They're quite personal," the headmaster says when she hands them to me. I take them gingerly, my arms still bound from wrist to elbow under my robes, my fingers gloved. The edges of the pages dig into me even so, my healing skin still sensitive. "You will scoff, I expect."

When she says nothing more, even in dismissal, I bow my head before turning to go. I've done my best to avoid her all these months, to avoid her office, but I always find myself drawn back here eventually, pinned to the golden mosaic of the sun pressed into the floor. One day, I'd planned to replace her, to claim this seat of power and influence for my own—but now, given the state of my hands, that feels further away than ever.

On my way back to my room, in an empty hallway down a twisting flight of stairs, I tuck the stack of letters under my arm and flex all my fingers. Some parts are forever dead to me, and any movement is still painful and slow. I can't hold a quill very well anymore, so Hadrian has been rewriting my class work. Using rune paint is difficult, but it can be done.

I remember to be glad I'm still alive.

With the weight of the letters heavy against my ribs, I almost don't notice Hadrian writing at our window seat, a book open in his lap, his face turned towards the sun. His arms are bare, his sleeveless tunic a sweeping swath of white that clings to his shoulders, the fabric tight across his chest. He turns when I enter, and just the sight of him calms me. He smiles, and I smile back.

Aware of his gaze on me, I spread the letters across my bed, choosing the first to read and arranging the rest by length. Each page is stained by fingerprints, the patterns entombed in smears of ink, almost as if the letters have been passed between many hands.

The penmanship is simple, but the writing is clear. *You've brought us such peace*, they promise me. *Thank you.*

I refold each letter along the crease lines when I'm done. There's a heaviness in the air, and it catches between my teeth.

No one's ever thought to send me a note of gratitude before. No king would ever dare. It makes knowing what I've done—what I *will* do, to feed the monster I'm indebted to—sit strangely with me for the first time in my life.

Even before the letters arrived, I'd been consumed by dreams of my old life: of the night I'd discovered I could hear the whispers of ghosts, of the day I'd passed the tests laid forth by the order, of the moment I'd revealed my potential as a lexicon mage—a rare but necessary combination for a phantom keeper.

I was eight when my father sold me into their service, when they started shaving my head, when they started stripping me bare and holding me down and painting every inch of my body to add to the reach of their spells.

For ten years, I had no choice and no say in anything that ever happened to me. I was beaten when I fought back, when I wore anything that exposed my skin, when I spoke out of turn. So I intoned their oaths, guarded their secrets, and helped them lie to both the living and the dead.

When I'd bound Elias, I'd only wanted to be free of it—of *them*. On the day we'd been hired to clear out his tomb, the order had tried to turn his ghost into a phantom. He'd fought the change, raging against the spell with strength that should've left him long ago. *I am stronger than death*, he'd said. *I have felled gods*.

I could see him back then, if only faintly; of all the ghosts I'd ever encountered, he was the only one with a visible form. Somber eyes, a lurid mouth, wide hands—they were features I could almost recognize, picked strategically, perhaps, to appeal to us. Even as a ghost, he had a presence more pervasive than any man I'd ever met.

He'd offered us magic beyond anything still seen in this world, but everyone else—my captors, my fellow prisoners— had turned a blind eye.

I had not.

The bow was all I'd had at hand; all I'd been allowed to carry for my own protection. So much of my skin had been covered with runes someone else had chosen, but one gap remained, a small secret I kept on my hip.

It was all I needed. That, and a splash of stolen rune paint.

We were nearly a hundred strong that day, our roles clear and divided: elders and apprentices, leaders and slaves. A thousand years of history, runes, spells, and discipline lived and died between these few.

Once I had caged Elias in my bow, just as any phantom could be trapped in a tiny glass vial, I struck down the members of the order one by one. Elias was stronger than them, stronger than all of them combined, and there was nothing they could do.

With his breath on my collar, the bow in my hands, he demanded I make phantoms of them all.

I watched them be devoured.

And I sealed my fate.

It's been a gruelling eleven years since then, and half a year since I last saw him, since that last ill-fated trip to Frostborro, and the days are getting shorter now. But as the nights grow darker, Elias grows restless, his anger polluting my mind. But finding the privacy to release one of the phantoms I've trapped is hard to come by; Elias's magic leaves its mark even if no one else can see him. A solution has yet to form in all the years I've been here, for all that I've scoured every corner of the academy's expansive grounds.

I'm beginning to wonder if I'm even truly looking for one at all.

Dimly, I notice the scratching of Hadrian's quill has quieted. Looking up, I find his gaze lingering on me. It's not unkind, his expression; instead, he looks puzzled. There's a peculiar tilt to his mouth that keeps my attention.

"You get this look on your face," he says airily, having to raise his voice just a little to carry across the room. It isn't a large space, but I've rearranged the furniture, obscuring the unfinished teleportation circle I'd drawn on the floor all those months ago. I've had no chance, no reason, to add the remaining runes, just as I've had no motivation to feed the monster whose powers I still struggle to use.

I eye the dressers between us, the beds, the desks, the chairs, and realize how much I hate that Hadrian feels so far away.

"What look?" I ask, humouring him.

"When you're thinking."

"Aren't I always thinking?"

Hadrian drops his chin onto his fist, his elbow resting on his upraised knee. Framed by the window, his back to the light, his warm brown skin is offset by the soft glow of the morning, his blond hair almost white.

He smiles, but I hear the question beneath his words. *What's bothering you?*

I set down the last letter, the paper suddenly fragile, the words flaking off the pages like ash.

I don't want to think about Frostborro anymore. I don't want to consider my place in their story, their tragedy. So instead, I ask, "If you think the academy is run by cowards, why do you stay?"

It's something that's been eating at me since we last spoke about this—about leaving. And suddenly, it's the most important thing I've ever wanted to know.

"I like your company," Hadrian says simply, readily, and there isn't a hint of deception in his voice.

I shake my head. "Other than that," I prod. "You don't stay imprisoned here just for me."

He seems to consider what else to say, and after a time, he sets down his book and his notes. He extends his legs, his knees bending over the edge of the window seat, and he plants his feet on the floor. I don't know why I track his movements so closely.

"I can control the fire now," he says, though it's more to himself than to me. "And we both know they won't kill me."

I nod. We've been over this before.

"So I have no reason to stay," he says, "besides you."

I scoff. I can't help it. The sound comes quickly and easily, the deflection automatic. "That can't be true."

He raises his brow, and with a softness that seems to warm the air, Hadrian says, "Is it so strange? To think I might be fond of you?"

I stare at him until my vision swims, until the light behind him entirely fades away, the sun swallowed by an oncoming storm.

I don't know when it begins to rain. At some point, I've looked away, back at the letters. I've sorted through them, reordered them. And still, we don't speak.

Eventually, Hadrian gets to his feet. He crosses the room to stand before me at the foot of my narrow bed.

"I was too forward," he says. "Forgive me. But you asked, and I told the truth."

"You'll have to leave one day," I tell him, even before he's finished speaking. "When your pride needs you. But I—I'll still be here."

I wonder, for a moment, if Hadrian might reach out to tip up my chin, but instead he rounds the bed and kneels in front of me, directly in my line of sight.

It's too much. It's not enough.

"Why do you stay?" he asks me. "What keeps the greatest mage of our generation caged in these halls? You could find a way to leave if you wanted to—I'm sure of it."

"I want to join the council," I say immediately. "I want to rule this place."

"As you deserve," he admits. "But why?"

The answer has never felt less clear. "Power, notoriety. There's no other way."

Hadrian hums at my feet, crossing his legs as he settles on the woven rug. He places his arms on my knees, leaning forward, looking up. The closeness is so intimate I can scarcely breathe.

"Pella," he says. Pea-la. The name cracks open something inside me. "Do you truly believe that?"

I hesitate. Why do I hesitate?

Hadrian smiles ruefully. "Do you remember the first time you saved my life?"

The answer comes easily, though the memory is distant and faded now. "I do." I'd taken a job out in the swamplands, visiting a small city on stilts after heavy rainfall had destroyed half the homes there in a flash flood. We'd been ambushed by a monster the size of a sea serpent, the creature's dangling headlamp as bright as the dawn. "Surely you're not attached to it."

"The part with the monster?" Hadrian asks, sounding bemused. "That's not what I meant." He shifts his weight, and his expression flickers to something wistful. "I'd been trapped at the academy for six years by then, and I was solemn about it, consumed with grief. It's the hardest thing I've ever survived. But I almost didn't. I didn't want to." His tone is even, unflinching, but the horror of what he's saying —of how close I'd come to losing him—hits me like an arrow to the chest. "And I wouldn't have, if not for you. I still don't know how you made the headmaster agree, but I've never forgotten that trip, or how it felt when you asked me to go with you."

Hadrian pauses before continuing. "You were *kind*," he says, and his voice emphasizes the word so heavily that it changes into something else. "You'd been going out on jobs for years and years and never once offered to take me. But I've always thought, somehow, you knew. That you saw what I needed when I needed it most. And being beyond the isles, even just for a little while...it made my life worth living again. It still does."

I stare at him. I can't help it. I don't know what I'd expected to see, but not this—not the tenderness on Hadrian's face, the gravity, the sincerity.

"You *help* people," he says softly. "It's what you do. Always. Even when something goes wrong, and things always go wrong, you never mind it."

He smiles again, and it's so small and secretive that it sends a pang through my heart. "You have more power than you know," he murmurs. "You don't need this place. You never have."

A hush falls over the room.

While my decisions have always felt self-righteous, self-motivated, my morals have always been clear. I don't gloat in front of the families of the dead because I promised myself I wouldn't; that I would separate what I do from what the order used to do. And I'm glad I helped Hadrian; I'm glad he's still here. Because I wouldn't want his half of the room being taken up by some stranger. Because he's intelligent and bright and deserves to see the wonders of the world again, beyond the walls and limits of this place.

Because I can't imagine what my life would look like without him.

And because I...

He—

Oh.

A rush of emotion I wasn't prepared for washes over me, so I look away from him. Across the room, I track the silver light flickering in the window, broken only by the heaviness of the rain.

Behind my eyes, I see the mines again, the tunnels, the colours that bled into lost souls. I remember how badly I'd wanted to find them, how determined I'd been, how softly I'd called out in answer to their sorrow, how carefully I'd drawn the teleportation circle to send them on.

I turn towards the letters on the bed. Seeing them makes me wonder if I've been sent others in the past, from other cities, other towns, but the headmaster deemed them too frivolous to see.

Or too dangerous.

It hits me, then. A realization so apparent it winds me. *Have I traded the order's control for the academy's?*

"I think I needed to hear that," I whisper, just as a roll of thunder cracks like a whip over the sea. "Thank you."

Hadrian waits until I meet his eyes again before extending his hand, and I take it. He squeezes my fingers. The burns are the worst there, on my right hand, but he's gentle with me—he always is. He kisses my knuckles, tender in a way that utterly shakes me. "You know I'm in love with you, don't you?" he says recklessly, fearlessly.

My heart stutters.

Dropping his gaze, Hadrian adds, "I've always hoped you'd leave with me one day. That you'd join my pride. You could still do your work as a phantom keeper if you travelled with me."

I want to laugh, but there isn't enough air in my lungs to manage it. I think I've lost track of what we're talking about.

When Hadrian looks back at me, I find his expression hasn't changed.

He says, "I know you. Parts of you. *This* part of you."

He reaches out, cradling my cheek in his hand. As always, his skin is warm, so warm.

"Pella," he says, and he says it, truly says it, carefully, openly, with all the right letters and sounds and meaning. Pea-la. My *name*. My chosen name. "You matter to me. To the world. When the time comes, leave with me. You are enough exactly as you are."

I lean into his palm, feeling something I've never felt before flicker to life in my chest. I've never known another soul like this, never had someone speak to me with such compassion and earnestness and care. Even the keepers, who would have kept me among their number until I died, hadn't bothered to know me, to begin to.

I look up at Hadrian as if I've never seen him before. Proud and bold, he's been both things since he was born, since the moment the lion inside him roared up to claim him, changing his skin and marking his body. But beyond those things, he's soft around the edges like rounded glass. If I touch him, I know my hands would slide across his body, around and around, a world without end. He is, in his heart, as he appears in my hands: hopeful, trusting, honest. He reflects who I am back at me, and I'm moved by the person he sees. Not the murderer, the recluse, the thief, the danger. He sees someone whole. Someone...*good*.

He sees me. The real me. Who I could be. Who I am. The words filter through my body from my head to my feet. I breathe in. I close my eyes.

When Hadrian leans in to kiss me, I let him. I feel the heat of his body as he moves closer, then the calluses on his fingers as he strokes my cheek. I smile, and he meets me. I meet him.

His mouth is as warm and careful as his words. The kiss is ginger, coaxing, and I tilt my head to allow space for his nose, for the press of his breath. He seems to fill the space all around me, expanding to reach the corners of my consciousness. I feel his chest meet my legs, his body folding around mine.

He holds me closer than anyone else ever has before. I'm made of straight lines and sheer valleys, shallow dips and sharp edges where the bones of my hips and my ribs meet my skin. I'm boxy and long, my shoulders strong, my chest flat, my body so far from delicate that it hardly knows the word at all. But here, pressed against him, I'm more than my body; I'm a soul, my soul, beyond the confines of my skin.

I part my lips, expecting Hadrian to sweep his tongue between them, but he hesitates. He pulls away. I see his face, so close his eyes distort for a moment, the flush of his cheeks so bright they illuminate the freckles around his nose, his cheekbones angular and high.

"Pella," he says. Oh, how the name changes me. Restores me. Revives me. "I...should've asked. Forgive me."

He pulls his hand from my face, the movement solemn and slow. I wonder if he thought I'd been about to speak, to ward him off, to push him away.

I ask, "Have you taken someone to bed before?"

His eyes focus on me—on the form that isn't there, not really, but must be. "I have experience, yes," he says. "With men and women both."

I remember to breathe, to think, to ground myself in the feeling of what I know: my name, the shape of my soul. I whisper, "For all that I am, I can't change how I look. What lies between my thighs is the truth of it."

"A truth," he says, and it's almost a question.

I smile then, bright and easy. "A truth," I agree. "I am

who I am. You're right; you're the only one who knows me. Truly knows me."

Hadrian holds out his hand. His skin is so dark in the dim light that he seems to dissolve into the shadows of the room. But when I touch his fingers, he is whole. For this moment more, he is mine.

"Ask, then," I murmur.

He draws to his feet, pulling me up with him. Gently, so gently, he rests his brow against mine, his other hand finding my waist, hooking into my clothes. His thumb brushes my skin, and I shiver at the nearness of it, almost closing my eyes again. But I want to see him. I want to see *this*.

"Be with me," he says, and it is reverent. Holy. "Do you desire it? Even just for one night?"

One. One. It echoes in my head a hundred, then a thousand times. *One night I can do. One night I can spare.*

"Yes," I whisper. "I do."

I do.

CHAPTER TEN

In Hadrian's bed, set by the window, he moves slowly, but with purpose. He eases me through the closeness as if he's afraid to startle me, kissing me soundly after each layer we leave on the floor. Boots, tunics, trousers, robes. There's a steady thrum of fabric whispering off our skin, the ties tangling at our feet.

I've dreamed of this, as much as I've denied it to myself. As much as I've fought it, lied about it, resisted it.

His sheets are cold, smelling faintly of lilies and lemongrass. As I lean back, his body bends over mine, and I sweep my hands across his chest, my gloves on the floor, my touch light and careful.

He's no king, my Hadrian, and no leader of his pride; not here, not yet. But he *is* my friend, and I trust him more than I can say.

I find I want to please him, and it's a feeling that comes easily.

Kissing his cheek, I guide him between my knees as I sit up on the edge of his bed. He stands, towering over me, almost unsure where to look. So I urge him closer, kissing the tip of his nose.

The privacy of our room is what truly gives us time; in any previous version of my life, I had none to give and none to share. Hadrian seems to understand the gravity of what I've offered him.

Gingerly, his hips slide against my thighs, his cock nudging against my skin. He is wide, unafraid of himself. It makes me eager to see how pleasure will shape his face.

I lift my right hand, his eyes watching where I go. I trail my fingertips over his stomach, then lower. "May I have you?"

He tilts up my chin with his finger, claiming my lips again as I fill my palm with the heat of him. The adrenaline eases the discomfort in my hand, but I welcome it even so. I stroke up, then back, then lick my fingers. Hadrian falters, turning his head away from me.

"You don't like it?" I ask him, pausing.

He looks back at me, and his blush is a pretty thing, pink along his ears. "I do," is what he says. "I just worry for your hands."

"What else are they for?"

He's warm; so warm to the touch that even his breath feels cool on my throat as he kisses me there. I tighten my grip, and he relaxes into the strokes like he's never known relief of this kind before. He moans against my shoulder, soft and sweet.

After some time of this, I push him back, just a little, and he goes. But when I try to slide to my knees at his feet, he catches my wrist, keeping me on the bed. "I won't last," he says with neither shame nor embarrassment. "Though I've wanted few things more."

Instead, he takes my hips and urges me back on the

71

sheets. He moves over my legs, his lips trailing up from my knee.

When the warmth of his mouth slides around my body, I cry out. Sharp, sudden, it's a burst of sound that surprises even me, and I muffle the next beneath my hand, though a low groan escapes even so.

No other partner of mine has ever done this; I've never allowed it. I don't like remembering which parts of my body I have and which I don't. It is horrid, in some ways, to feel anything at all. But with Hadrian, there's no question of *why*. Why it doesn't shape who I am—and never has.

I feel fully realized, to be explored like this. Hadrian's mouth slides languidly from the tip to the base of me, engulfing me, swallowing what leaks from his touch. I lose all sense of time, and only my grip on his shoulders grounds me to this moment. When I nudge the back of his throat, he lingers, and tears begin to pool in the corners of my eyes. I thread my fingers through his hair, tugging at him, and he stays; he chooses to stay. I make a mess of his mouth before he pulls away.

His absence is like a spear pulled from my body. I feel jagged, torn open, and helpless. I reach for him, and he holds me until the feeling fades, until the fear slips away.

"I'm here," he says, one of his arms wrapped loosely around my waist, and I nod. He squeezes my hand, forever gentle with me. "Is it too much?"

I rub my eyes with my other hand. The burns on my second and fourth finger glint in a flash of lightning. *I feel alive* is what I most want to say.

"Everything's different with you," I whisper instead, and when he smiles, I'm awash with a feeling so strange I wonder if I might die here, in his arms, in his bed.

Placing his knee on the bed, he eases himself over my

body again, draping a long shadow over my chest and legs. He pins me down, careful with the weight of him, and the bed groans with the addition. The animal behind his eyes comes alive, each iris reflecting something bright and true.

"I've hoped for this," he says, sliding a hand between us, lifting one of my knees, and circling the tight ring of muscle at the base of my spine. "I could write poetry about you."

The thought utterly embarrasses me. "Don't you dare."

He smiles mischievously. "You've never wondered how your body moves in the moonlight? How your hips tangle with the warmth of the sun? How your—"

"Hadrian." It isn't a curse; it isn't even a refusal. Not really. "Please."

I kiss him then, with both my hands on his cheeks, holding him while he eases me open. He spits on his hand to help with the tension, but then he reaches for something in a drawer in the small table by his bed.

This makes things easier, and my hands wander to his back when he repositions himself, his chest arching over mine. My eyes flutter open and closed, my mouth forming words I can't quite understand. He kisses the curve of my throat, the sweep of my collar, then circles both peaks on my chest with his tongue. His attention is a kind of magic all on its own.

When he removes his fingers, he gauges my reaction, and I feel ready. I shift my legs, wondering if he'll flip me onto my stomach, if he'll bury my voice in his pillow. I wait, but he doesn't move.

"Your face," he finally says, bemused by the confusion that flits across my expression. "I'd like to see it."

Ah. Somehow, that makes me feel even more exposed than I already am.

The room is dark, so dark, when Hadrian slides against

me, just barely nudging our bodies together. I anchor my feet behind him, on either side of his hips, and my arms feel impossibly long, my elbows resting on his shoulders, my fingers tangling in his hair. I see the moment as if suspended in time, the muscles in his legs trembling, his dark skin burning in answer to everything I touch.

His lips find mine, and I allow it, this vulnerability. I'm few of the things I've told him—a great mage, a great archer —but I *am* Pella. *I am Pella.*

Hadrian doesn't push. He eases himself forward, so slowly there is no pain. I pull him closer, his hips stuttering at my urgency. He sinks in, deeper and deeper, moaning at the feeling of it.

"You're so warm," he says, and it's breathless. He's breathless. "I'll remember that."

He starts moving then, with a steady, easy pace that blisters into my memory, and it makes me smile, seeing how he enjoys himself. It reminds me to be present, to concentrate on my body in a way I never have before. I follow the ghost of his hands on my sides, on my arms; I trace over where he kisses me, where his mouth goes, where he presses hard against my skin. I beg for marks, and he leaves them, teasing me with his teeth wherever I ask. He leaves me trembling, gasping, my hands scrabbling for an anchor to this moment. I've carved a constellation into his back, I'm sure, the lines shallow and red.

I don't remember saying his name, but I must have, his eyes snapping to mine. He blushes, flustered and overcome, and I suddenly can't bear the thought of not telling him how I feel, how I've opened myself to the weakness he's created in me. "I love you too," I whisper, and the words alone knock me senseless.

Hadrian parts his lips, begging for my confession again, echoing it, and I am lost.

He groans when he finishes, blinded by it, the sound not fully human. And I keep him there, with me, for as long as he'll have me.

Afterwards, as he winds down, his face buried in the crook of my shoulder, his breath sticky on my skin, he kisses me again. The touch lingers; the feeling burns.

When he slips from me, he is careful; he keeps one hand between us, moving slowly. Then he lays in the sheets beside me, our hands finding each other.

I curl into him. I can't help it.

"I want more," he says, his nose in my hair. I still at the words. "I'll always want more. Will you think on it?"

I know the right answer—I have to say no. I should. But I *also* want more; more of him, more of this. More of my life as...Pella.

But I can't think of the words to express that just now, to give shape to how much I want to stay here, at the academy —and equally, how much I want to leave. I can't think past the pleasant feeling in my legs and the ache in my chest. Perhaps I'm distracted by the weight and the heat of him, so the answer is biased anyway. Fleeting.

So for now, all I can do is hold him, his heart against mine, and dream.

CHAPTER ELEVEN

Maybe I could change things, if I stayed, is the new thought that comes to me on the lazy days, the cold nights, the amber mornings, when Hadrian dozes soundly with his head on my chest. *With power, I could change everything about this place.*

But do I want to?

It's a question that lingers with me, forever in the air. Though there are few places to ruminate between my endless classes and Hadrian's bed—where one night together becomes two, and then four, and then a number I lose track of suddenly, willingly, all at once.

But in the hours before first light one day, I find myself restless, possessed, indecisive.

There's a shared bath down the hall from our room, the water in the recessed pool often cold, the mirrors polished, the curtains steamed. It's meant to be used for refreshment, meditation, or a quick wash—not laps. But after slipping from Hadrian's grasp, I find myself alone there. Who would stop me?

The water isn't deep; it sloshes against my stomach when I stand near the middle, and hits just above my ribs when I drift to either end. The chill is soothing on my healing skin, but I can't swim with bandages on. So it's always a risk, coming here, as much as it's a balm.

Still, I seize my moment of peace, and when my head clears enough to let me think, when the memory of Hadrian's hands fades from my skin, I rest with my back against the edge of the pool, my reflection slowly forming on the water as it stills. My hair is growing out, and my lips look softer, redder. Well kissed.

I've never been in love before, but I decide I like the look of it. It makes me wonder if I could ever learn to love *myself*.

I trace the slope of my jaw with the fingertips of my left hand, where I can still feel something. I trace my nose, my chin, then the dip below my throat, thumbing the thick bone waiting there. I wander lower, along my sternum, over the flat planes of my chest. Lower still, to my boxy waist, my hips, then the tops of my thighs.

I could change how some of this looks, if I wanted to. I could work to hide the muscle. I could almost have curves, faint but pleasing, if I dressed in different robes, pulled my belt tight in a different place. If I tried, I could create the illusion of a body that would suit me. Honour me.

Or—

I lift both my hands, letting my eyes fall to the scarring along my forearms. I look, *really* look, and try to accept what I see. The white, twisting ropes of skin that will never lay flat, the dead spots and stretches of flesh that are ashen and grey. They are a part of me now. All of it.

I pretend to draw my bow, my arms flexing, my body

falling into place on memory alone. I imagine the wood in my hand, the string against my fingertips, the feathers of an arrow against my cheek. I adjust my form, turn my hips. I imagine Elias, rage behind his eyes, demanding a sacrifice.

I loose the arrow. There is no sound, no weapon. But I watch it fly past the walls of this room, past the drop at the edge of the isle, past the ones below.

I wonder, dimly, how Hadrian and I could ever escape this place. The gondolas won't take us without a team to turn the gears, and the drop alone, straight to the sea, would surely kill us. Even the nearest, closest isle is too far away to reach by any means we have access to.

And there is always the matter of our vials of blood.

Turning my back on the academy would also mean forgoing over a decade of hard work. Relationships with royal courts, fees and education I've paid for, teachings I've been promised, spells I'll never learn anywhere else. My dreams of ruling, of reshaping this world from the highest seat of power, will be lost.

But you also won't be trapped here, I remind myself. *You'd be free.*

But free to do what?

Admitting I've managed to trick myself into trading one prison for another, the order for the academy, is one thing. But if I leave with Hadrian, wouldn't living amongst his pride be more of the same?

Returning to our room, I consider grabbing a few things and leaving, retreating somewhere to study, but Hadrian is still asleep. And something about seeing him so still, so peaceful, makes me envious.

I crawl back into his bed, tucking my legs behind his. I whisper into his hair, "Would you leave your pride for me?"

He doesn't answer, his snores light and soft, but the

image won't let me go. So I promise myself, there and then, that I won't leave the academy for another cage, to become a part of something else. I want something *new*. Something all my own.

If I decide to destroy my dreams of power, another must take its place. It's only right.

I give up on studying after eating a warm breakfast, the bread rolls fresh, the butter newly churned. All the students at the academy are made to eat together, pressed closely around tables arranged in endless rows. We have some choice in the food we eat, but not in the hour or the amount we're served.

Some of the students need this place, I know. Some of them, like Hadrian, have powers and magic that aren't easy to control. So the academy still serves a purpose, for all that I hate it, and young mages will die without the direction, protection, and guidance offered here.

That doesn't mean it isn't a prison—just that I can't tear down its walls. I'd have to replace it first; replace the role it serves.

I've considered, in the past, what I'd need to do to take over the academy by force. And while I could find a way to kill the headmaster, the councillors are hidden among the instructors here; I wouldn't want to kill them all.

And there are spells, enchantments, curses, and precautions carved into the very floorboards here, into the stairwells, the doorways, the ceilings, the walls. I can guess what they do, though I'm not entirely sure.

I'd have to sink all four of the isles to remake this place, to offer a means to easily stay or go. But nothing would survive the fall.

It's a wider mission for another day. Today, there's only one thing I can do and one thing I can control.

I take to the archery field, careful to choose a lane far enough away from other students to hide how badly my hands struggle with the draw. The targets are set up at equal distance across the lawn, the high walls surrounding the grounds casting a long shadow over the grass. It cuts the wind, but at the start and end of each day, it blocks the light. For some, this is a hindrance. For me, merely a distraction.

Elias doesn't speak when I string my bow, though he appears just to the right of me, materializing on the grass. He regards my scars as if he can see them under my clothes, then watches me hook my quiver to my waist, and waits.

Then, abruptly, he says aloud, "You test my patience."

His voice is like listening to a gondola as it grinds along its ropes, or the sound of an animal screeching. I flinch, and it reveals why he's bothered speaking to me like this at all.

I eye the next nearest archer standing a handful of paces away. She shoots at the farthest target, misses, and then leaves her place to retrieve all the arrows she's used. I turn to Elias then, facing him head on.

"I need your help."

He cocks his head. "You always do."

He's taller than usual today, I realize. His features are slightly distorted, his eyes further apart, his mouth wider, his jaw sharper, as if he's forgotten how to be entirely human in the time he's spent growing hungrier and hungrier. His hair is longer, hanging past his shoulders, and it's black as ash. He wears armour, styled like a battle mage, his chest plate branded with an axe, the metal gleaming and dark. He could strike me at the temple with just his hand and shatter my skull.

For all the reasons I have to leave this place, I can't leave *him*. I can't let the bow fall into someone else's hands.

I fire an arrow—just one. It hits the nearest target, but only the outer ring. My arm guard digs painfully into my flesh as the string strikes the leather, throwing my aim. It's a wonder I can hit anything at all. My hands shake from the effort of gripping the bow tightly and curling my fingers so close to a fist.

I ask him simply, "Could you fly us out of here?"

Elias laughs, the sound harsh and unforgiving. "I'm no beast of burden."

I nod. "Only a man of opportunity." I fire another arrow, ignoring the searing pain in my hands. "If I'm free of this place, I could kill for you."

He eyes me then, beneath his pitch-black brows. "You could kill for me here. Now. You could kill her."

He points at the nearest archer. Then the one past her, and the one past *her*.

"I won't kill another student."

"Why? If you intend to leave, what does it matter?"

I think of the two phantoms I still have hidden in my room and how much they haunt me. I know, if pressed, I could offer him one of those. But then I think of the letters from Frostborro, the families, the fingerprints, the names. I close my eyes.

I fire three more shots into the quiet. I squint, focusing my aim, but still miss the center mark. Elias watches me fail, bemused. "You're little without me, boy," he says.

Girl. I lower the bow. My arms burn. My hands burn. "I'm the last phantom keeper," I tell him. "And you *will* help me, or I won't help you."

It's an idle threat—and he knows it. "You need my power," he says bluntly. "Even if it's just to impress your kings."

It sounds pathetic, when he says it, but those accolades had motivated me for so long. I bow my head. "I'll wait you out," I threaten. "You will suffer."

His voice is cold. "So be it then."

CHAPTER TWELVE

Hadrian doesn't like my plan. What I tell him of it, anyway. "You're just...going to ask the headmaster for our vials back," he says, sounding perplexed. "Do you really think that will work?"

He crosses his arms, the shirt he's chosen hanging low on his body, revealing parts of his chest as he moves. At his feet, he's already begun packing his bag, the inner lining watertight, a folio of papers and a few books he's chosen to steal from the library tucked between a change of clothes. From that alone, I know he has faith in me.

"If it's that easy," he continues, "wouldn't everyone try to leave?"

I don't want to tell him I'll have to threaten the headmaster. I don't want to tell him the plan entirely depends on the godkilling ghost in my bow deciding to help me—help *us*. I don't want to tell him I'll have to reveal one of the most closely guarded secrets I've kept all these years: that I'm a murderer.

So I decide not to tell him any of that.

Instead, I take his face in my hands. He preens under

the attention, sitting up straighter at the edge of his bed. Then he tries to pull me into the ruffled sheets behind him, smiling at the distraction, his eyes dropping to the bite mark I know mars the side of my throat.

His tiny bed isn't built for two, but I gave up keeping my own neat and orderly some weeks ago, my pillow now permanently next to his.

"I need you to trust me with this," I tell him, resisting the pull. "It *will* work."

He tilts up his chin, regarding me from beneath his long lashes, his lips rosy.

"Alright," he says, his arms relaxing their grip around my waist. The glass bottles along the windowsill on his left catch the light, covering him in swathes of colour. "Is there anything I can do to help?"

There is, but I can't tell him what I need just yet; not until every other part of the plan is in place. We have to wait for a delivery day, when I know a merchant ship from the continent will be bringing supplies to the lower isles, like bandages, ink, metal, and clothes. That will be our only means of escape across the sea, assuming we make it to the harbour.

One step at a time.

I lean down to kiss him, coaxing open his mouth. Hadrian groans, trying to pull me into his lap, but I brace myself on his shoulder, holding him back. "You wound me," he says, but catches my bottom lip between his teeth. "You mean to ask me something serious."

"I do," I reply. I kiss him again for good measure, then drop my hand into the neck of his shirt. He shivers. "Is it working? Am I weakening your resolve?"

His eyes are glassy, perhaps even a little unfocused. But

when he blinks, the moment passes, and his vision clears. He sobers.

"Ask," he says. "Break my heart, if you must."

I wonder if he means that in jest, but he doesn't laugh. His expression never changes.

I sit down heavily on the bed beside him. "Would you leave your pride for me?"

Hadrian furrows his brow in response, taking me in, his forearms balanced on his knees. His hands come together, gripping his fingers tightly. He searches my face for an explanation I haven't offered.

I want to say, *your father is young*. I want to say, *you have a brother who could lead in your stead*. But I know his pride is important to him, and for all that he's lingered at the academy for me, there's never once been any pressure to return, any reason to go back on any specific day in all the years he's been here.

Eventually, he says, "Where else would we go?"

I lay out my thoughts on my open hands. I've had six weeks to think about it—six weeks; forty-two days; just over a thousand hours. I've hardly slept, and when I do, I've dreamed of this, dreamed of my plan.

"We would form a band or a group," I explain, "of enchanters, scholars, and mages. We would work to replace the need for the academy."

Hadrian breathes in. He regards me seriously, weighing the options in his own open hands as if they have real, palpable weight.

After a while, he draws away from me, moving across the room, around it. He paces, circling the floor. His energy is contagious.

"It's daring," he says, returning to me. I think I see a glimmer of excitement in his eyes.

"Do you think you could teach other fire mages how to control their power?" I ask. "There was a world before the academy was formed. Magic must have existed. Mages would have found a way to survive."

Hadrian takes my hands in his, holding me firmly but gently. He squeezes my palms. I squeeze his back.

"Until my father passes," he says at last, agreeing for now. "Can we revisit this then?"

It's the best answer I could've hoped for. "Of course."

On the night of our escape, Hadrian helps me roll all the remaining pots of rune paint between strips of our bedsheets, torn to make padding for the glass. There are six in total, enough to paint my entire body a few times over, each pot about the size of my hand. This is everything I've managed to save over the years for personal use, scraped from inkwells and requisitions when I was ordered just barely enough for the tasks I'd been assigned.

There's one other on my desk that I've been using, but there's only a small splash of rune paint still inside, the liquid illuminated by a small candle set next to it, Hadrian's smokeless fire a dark blue.

"Can I help with anything else?" Hadrian asks again, for maybe the fifth time, and I know I can't delay the inevitable any longer.

"You should sleep," I suggest, motioning to his bed, "while I finish painting. It's all I have left to do."

Hadrian's eyes drink me in, sincere and unsuspecting. He nods, bending to kiss my cheek before he tucks himself away.

"I could do more," he says, but he's already drowsy. He's

been up with me, preparing, for the last two days. "Don't be afraid to wake me if you change your mind."

I don't have the heart to lie to him again, so I don't say anything at all.

I wait almost an hour to be sure he's asleep, his snores soft and rumbling, before I crouch over a small bowl of cloudy water I place on the floor by our window, a curved blade pressed to the side of my throat. The metal is cold, so cold it stings when it touches my skin. In the quiet, it's easy to forget what I'm about to do.

My hair is wet, and the ends stick to the skin under my chin like a noose. It's just long enough to ghost above my shoulders, and it's the longest it's ever been; the longest I've ever allowed it to grow.

Raising the blade, I scrape along the fine hairs at the base of my scalp, watching as tiny black curls fall into the bowl. But when I move the blade higher, the sharp edge guided by feeling and touch alone, I panic. My hands are shaking, and each breath slips over my lips with a hitch and a stutter. The blade catches on my skin, slicing deep, and I drop it, as much from surprise as from pain.

There's blood on my fingers, and now there's blood on the floor. It's bright red, burning hot, and seeing it makes my head spin. The room tilts sharply to the right, my heart suddenly pounding so hard I can feel it smacking against my ribs, the pain engulfing my chest.

I close my eyes—and instantly, I'm a child again. Ten. Twelve. Fourteen. Eighteen. A knife, cold and sharp, just like the one I'd held in my hand, drags thoughtlessly around my ears, over my head, and down my neck. I can feel my hair being cut out in handfuls, the strands dropping onto my legs, trickles of blood running down my back. And on my arms, I feel the ghost of cruel, wandering hands, the pressure moving over my body as someone older than me, stronger, holds me down while I struggle, trying to get away.

The memories are so loud that they rattle inside my body, and I just barely manage to keep them from seeping out between my teeth.

By the time the terror passes, the room has grown dark, the candle on the desk blowing out, a passing cloud swallowing the light of the moon. The concoction I'd rubbed into my hair has dried stiff and tacky, and when I raise my eyes, the bed across the room from me is empty. Hadrian is no longer there.

Somewhere in the time I've lost, he's moved to stand in front of me, making his way around the furniture I've pushed against the walls, around the bags he and I have finished packing.

I meet his eyes, his piercing green eyes, and he kneels on the floor. I don't know how long he's been watching me, trying to decide how best to help. "I'm here," he says softly.

When I don't move any closer, he pulls back, but only a little. "What happened?" he asks me, eyeing where my blood has dried on the floor. When I still don't reply, he tries again. "What did you do?"

The lie falls out of me, incomplete and wrong. "I was shaving."

"The back of your head?" He picks up the blade, the edge serrated and long. "With this?"

I realize, only then, that half of my body has gone numb. I try to uncurl my legs, but everything juts away from me when I try. I start shaking again.

Hadrian gazes at where I've painted my skin. My legs, shoulders, and upper arms are all crowded with silver runes. I'm in nothing but my smallclothes, so he can see exactly where I started to paint and where I stopped, how high the runes reach on my ribs, how close I've had to pack them along the sides of my throat. I've never let him see them before; not like this, not in their entirety. I try to cover myself, and his eyes flash back to my face. "You were cutting your hair," he suggests.

The truth hits me like a spear.

"Hadrian," I say quietly, finding the strength to speak while I stare at the floor. I'm not ashamed, though I loathe my own weakness; sacrifice used to come so easily to me. "I...need the room to paint. That's all."

He's slow to understand. He blinks, looking first at my scars, at the skin raised and puckered around my knuckles, then all the way down to my elbows. When I flex my fingers, he seems to see it all at once—my ravaged skin is too uneven to hold the shape of any runes.

His thoughts are loud in the quiet of the room. His guilt burns bright across his face, horrid and misshapen, twisting the lines around his eyes and mouth.

I say what I always say when we're reminded of this—of what happened. "It wasn't your fault."

"It was. It is," he says. His voice breaks. "I can't fix it. But I *can* help."

Hadrian moves. He holds out his hand, his arm, his skin bare from shoulder to fingertip. The movement makes no sound, but the offer shatters the silence that has completely flooded the room.

I suck in a breath.

"Use me as you need," he says. "Please."

A canvas. His *body*. The mere thought settles somewhere high in my throat, choking me. The trust he'd have to place in me, and the trust *I'd* have to place in *him*, almost kills me to consider.

I'd have to cover him in spells I've never let anyone else

see—that I've always hidden from him. I'd have to show him the heart of what it means to be what I am, what it means to be a phantom keeper.

And *he'd* have to trust *me* to break them, to wash away the runes with a smear of my blood. Without that, the paint would permanently mar his body, able to be used again and again. He'd become a vessel, a talisman, a grimoire, a slave, as useful to any other lexicon mage as I'd once been to the order. I still carry the horror of that time, when my skin was reduced to nothing but material, an extension of another man's will.

How could I willingly do that to someone else? To someone I *love*?

"I want to," Hadrian says suddenly, and I realize I've taken his hands. "I want to help. Let me help you."

Let me help you.

It's too much. *He's* too much.

I pull him towards me. The small bowl of water splashes over my lap, the blue ceramic rattling against the floor. I wrap my arms around his neck, burying my face in his hair.

He's asking me to trust him with everything I am. This is more than my body, my past—this is my *future*. Even if I can look beyond my own trauma, if he turns around and takes the spells to the headmaster, I'm through. Between the teleportation circle I've drawn on the floor of this room and the spells I'll have to paint on his skin, that's everything that makes me a phantom keeper; and in the hands of someone else, everything I've destroyed—the order, my life—would be meaningless. *I* would be meaningless.

I can't do it. *I can't.*

"It's a risk," is what I say instead. I can barely manage it.

He replies, "So is love. But that's what we're doing, isn't it?"

He's asking me for the impossible, this gloriously wonderful, stupidly impulsive, ridiculously open-hearted man. But I can't tell him how close he is to the truth.

Because he's right. In this, he's always been right.

"If I trust you with this," I whisper to him, conceding, "then we're in this together. Promise me, Hadrian."

His breath is warm on my cheek. "Until the gods call me home," he says, "I promise."

The sun hasn't risen just yet, but when I finish painting Hadrian's chest, my fingertips stained with silver, we both know it's time to go. Our satchels are packed, our room stripped, our beds bare, our books properly stored. But for now, we'll have to leave all of that behind.

"Are you ready?" he asks, watching me dress, the runes on my body carefully covered by my robes. In comparison, he's pulled on only a tunic and a loose pair of trousers, his boots tucked under his bed.

"As I'll ever be," is my reply. I can't bring myself to look at him again. It'll remind me of what I've done, what I've accepted, what I've decided to risk.

Hadrian follows me through the wings and halls of the academy that we'll never see again. Past classrooms and galleries, exhibition spaces and study rooms, past the archive, the library, the great hall, the aviary. There's little we don't see on our route to the headmaster's office.

The door is slightly ajar when we arrive, as it always is. In truth, I'm not sure if she sleeps.

I pause, coming up short, turning to Hadrian. Everything is going exactly as I'd hoped. I motion to him, and he nods. Then he shifts.

There's a step between human and animal that Hadrian's mastered, his shoulders growing fur, his feet and hands forming claws. His hair becomes a mane, his ribs bending out like a birdcage. But through all the change, I can still see his face.

There are fewer bones to break this way, less agony, less pain. But he also has less power. He's taller than me, stronger, broader, but he's no mythical lion.

"Stay here," I whisper, "like this. Stay threatening. I need you to guard the door."

He eyes me. The bones in his face have rearranged, but his irises are the same, green and dazzling. We hadn't discussed this part of the plan since I knew he'd hate it.

I take a deep breath. "And don't come in, no matter what you hear. If I need you, I'll come for you."

Hadrian's expression is hard to read. He looks at the crack of light slipping around the headmaster's door, then back at me. Finally, he nods. But before I turn to go, he takes my hand in his...hand? Paw? I stare at it. I almost can't believe it belongs to my friend. He has leathery pads under his palm and along each finger like a lion would, and his claws are long.

"Nothing is worth your life," he says simply, "if it comes down to it."

"This *will* work," I reply. "Have a little faith."

He lets me go. But I feel his eyes on me every step of the way.

Walking into the headmaster's office requires no preamble. I don't knock. I don't announce myself. I just shut the door quietly behind me.

She raises her head. "I wasn't expecting you," she says.

She's sitting at her desk, the dark wood covered in scrolls and quills and paperwork, some of the ink running red and blue and black under her hands as she switches between tasks. "Why are you here?"

She's perfectly calm. She's spent her life training to be. I cross the room, and she eyes the quiver on my back, my bow strung, but doesn't ask.

"We're leaving," I announce airily. "Hadrian and I."

She drops her eyes to her work. "Braver men than you have tried."

I walk closer to her desk. She smells faintly of rosewater, her hair slightly damp and pulled behind her head in a loose bun. She looks younger than she is, the cut of her robes sitting high and tight on her body, the collar enclosing her neck. Her hair is grey only at the temples, her lips pert, her eyes keen.

She doesn't look up again for some time. When she does, she seems genuinely surprised to see I'm still standing there. She sets down her quill.

"I want the vials of our blood you keep on file."

"Your phylacteries," she says, then tuts. "No."

I put my hand on the edge of her desk, crumpling a map she'd been drawing on. She tracks the movement, visibly annoyed, but does nothing to stop me.

"We both know you won't kill Hadrian."

At this, she raises one of her brows, bemused. I want to smack the expression right off her face. She leans back, and her throne-like chair, carved from redwood and painted with gold gilt, groans ominously. "I can kill anyone at this academy," she insists. "I'm dangerously close to killing you."

"You can't."

She smiles, all teeth. "Do explain why you think so."

Outside, the world begins to fill with colour. The

sunrise is pale today, the sky cold, the darkness slow to retreat.

The headmaster is framed by four massive windows, two on either side of her desk, but directly behind her is a stretch of stone wall. She's put up a plaque, but I can't read it from here. I've memorized everything else about this room.

I let her think I've lost steam. I stall, biting my lip, then glance back at her, affecting nonchalance.

The moment has come.

"I'm the last phantom keeper."

There's a pause, heavy and drawn out, and I half expect her to laugh, though I've never seen it happen. I know such a claim should sound outrageous. The order was well established, overly cautious, and powerful. There's no world where all the other phantom keepers could've died in some catastrophe.

But she doesn't laugh. Her mouth pulls tight, her jaw clenching.

"Prove it," she says, breathing out the words. But she hesitated too long; I already know she believes me.

Eleven years of requests for my services as a phantom keeper have come to her. I know they have—people die tragically all the time, almost every day. And despite how few of those jobs she's ever accepted, or allowed *me* to accept, it would've been obvious from the letters that the order never acted, even when the requests were well paid.

And then there's the matter of my enrolment here, at the academy. It's strange that the order would agree to it—to losing one of their own. And they've never complained about the academy advertising my presence for their own gain. It's never happened before and hasn't happened since.

She must now realize I was never given permission.

I whisper the truth. "I killed them. All of them."

Her eyes study my face.

I step back from her desk. "Give me the vials."

She crosses one of her legs over the other, her expression unreadable, but I can tell she's unsettled. She's pulling inward, towards her chest. She crosses her arms.

"You think I won't kill you," she says evenly, "if you're the last."

"A thousand years of knowledge and secrets, traditions and work. I'm the only one who knows how any of it is done." I motion to her. "You're an academic, a historian. You wouldn't risk that loss. What would the world be without phantom keepers?"

She considers this, tapping her lip, her expression serious and stern. But her eyes don't leave mine. She's pretending to be unmoved. "No."

I already know where she keeps the vials; she took my blood all those years ago in this very room, and then stepped through the door in the wall to the right of her desk. Why keep something secret when the door is enchanted? When she's so assured of total control?

I don't want to threaten her—this will be messier if I do. "Do you expect me to just return to my room?" I ask, trying again. The new angle bewilders her, the tension in her jaw going slack. "You'll never be able to let me leave again. You'll have to turn down every request that comes in. No matter who asks for me—kings, queens, mayors, priests— you'll have to refuse them, all while the dead wail at their doors. And in all the years that pass, what do you think I'll do here? Why would I play nice?"

She rises from her chair. "Do you think," she says slowly, "that I don't know most of the students here wish to leave? The Academy of Light isn't built on the willing, on the just. If you value your life, you'll fall back in line."

I draw my bow, pointing an arrow at her chest. "Give me the vials."

She looks at the weapon, staring down the threat, then sits back in her seat. She holds out her hands. "Even if you kill me, the door you wish to open is enchanted by the council. You'll have to find and kill every member. You don't even know how many there are, and everything inside is enchanted the same way."

Elias appears at my side, my grip on my bow tightening. He's been left to languish for nearly a year, growing hungrier by the day, and the changes in his face reveal his failing grasp on his human form. His mouth stretches so far back along his jaw that it almost reaches his ears. His eyes are slits, his teeth sharp, his skin translucent and grey.

"You're wasting your time," he says, his voice mangled and harsh. "Kill her." But I ignore him.

I step around the desk, aiming my bow at the soft palate of her throat. Still, she does nothing.

There's magic written on every inch of her skin, I'm sure. Protections and cures, defences and curses. But she hesitates. I know she wants what she can sell, what she can hawk to anyone who can pay. And I'm powerful, likely the most powerful student she's ever had and *will* ever have. She would regret my loss, my death. Perhaps I really would've been raised to the council one day.

She needs me to cooperate.

"You could split your time," she offers. "Spend half of it here, at the academy."

"Why even bother?"

"You can't leave forever," she says. My arms begin to

tremble; I can't hold the weight of this full draw much longer. "The other students can't know that it's possible."

I grit my teeth. "Will you give me more than the vials?"

Her eyes narrow. "What more would you want?"

I see the lure for what it is, but I can't resist the call. *I have to know what she thinks my life is worth.*

"A seat on the council," I demand. "And Hadrian is free to go."

Her eyes flicker to the door behind me. "What would I say," she asks, "to explain where he's gone?"

"I don't care," I lie. "We can claim he was killed. I can say it was a monster."

Her stare is hard—harder than ice, harder than steel. "He must never speak about the academy outside these walls," she spits out. "If he does, I'll kill him myself." Her tone is flat, but the threat is serious. I don't doubt she has a way to keep track of such things. "And I must always know where you are, even when you're here. You will answer to no one but me."

I lower my bow, my hands and shoulders burning. "The vials. Once I see them, I'll agree. Those are my terms."

She stands again. "Very well."

As she walks to the enchanted door, the magic etched into the wood responding to her touch, I'm suddenly confronted with a choice. I could shoot her the moment she opens it; I could shoot her the moment she turns her back. Or...I could choose not to shoot her at all. I could accept what she's offered. I could live exactly the life I've always wanted.

I raise my bow as the door opens. But she moves far faster than I expect.

When the door shuts firmly behind her, I realize I've

been played. Elias must realize it too. He laughs, the sound inhuman. Ungodly.

I count the passing seconds in my head. She can kill me the moment my vial of blood touches her hand. How long do I have?

Elias leans close. "I win, then," he says, pleased with the chance to goad me, to show me that, in the end, he was right —I do need him more than he needs me. "I always win. You need my power. You're useless without it."

"You have to stop her," I tell him.

"You know the price," he replies, his voice gravelly.

I draw my bow.

I fire.

The door to the room of phylacteries blows open in an explosion of light, the boom deafening, the arrow engulfed by the black miasma that always seeps out of Elias's shifted form. He transformed into a crow so quickly I missed it, his massive talons smashing through the thick, ancient wood, the hinges melting, the enchantments destroyed. Within, the splintered debris slams into a glass cabinet, but nothing breaks. The other spells hold.

At the same time, the headmaster screams.

I step inside.

I find myself looking at rows and rows of enchanted glass, each display case containing perhaps a hundred hanging vials of blood all the length of my hand. Each shelf is marked with a letter, each vial inscribed with a name.

The headmaster is crushed beneath a part of the door, her legs mangled, her chest caving in.

In her hand are both vials, the glass perfect, the corks untouched.

Her next breath comes out as a wheeze. "You're a fool," she says.

"I was never going to stay," I reply.

I shoot through her face.

Her head snaps back and her hair splatters against the wall. The blood and gore are bright red and black, bits of bone blown across the floor.

I only have a moment. I extend my hand, burning the spell I've written on my chest and legs.

The ghost of her, seeping from her mouth, turns blue.

I've only seen this once before—watched a living soul become a dying one in real time. For all the people I've killed, all the keepers that died at my hand, only the last could be made into a phantom this quickly, all the other bodies dropping where they fell, their ghosts allowed to fill the space in Elias's tomb. That phantom had been purple, glorious and bright. The headmaster's is dull, as if coloured by shock.

I pull a small vial from my belt, sweeping the phantom behind the glass. The spell I've painted on my neck burns away with a vengeance.

Behind me, I can feel Elias's eyes on my hands. But when I turn to face him, the Elias I know is no longer there. His body has doubled over, his spine seeming to arch out of his back. His arms have gotten longer, his mouth wider, his skin darker.

It looks like he's melting.

His human form twists into something made entirely of bone and tar. His eyes are still green, but his face is grotesque, his hands dragging on the floor, his knees bent under his body, his jaw snapping apart from his skull, skeletal wings growing from beneath his shoulders.

His hunger is like a living thing slithering from his mouth.

"You want it?" I ask him.

His gaze flickers to the right before slamming into mine. He screams, and it's ear-splitting. Monstrous. Uncanny. It's like listening to a death rattle, like hearing someone being crushed to death underfoot.

The anger in his glare could blot out the sun.

"Boy," he says. "You *owe* me. That was our bet. Our *deal*."

He's never scared me before; not really. Not like *this*.

I throw the headmaster's vial across the room, and when it hits the ground, it shatters. I lift my bow, nocking an arrow again, and fire through the little wisp of colour that dances into the light.

Elias falls upon the phantom in shifted form with a ravenous shredding sound—as if there's something there to tear into, to crunch on, to devour. He chews and rips and bites at nothing I can understand.

I walk out of the headmaster's office, my bow slung over my shoulder and neck, the string across my back. Hadrian is sitting on the floor. He looks up when he sees me, and I shut the door so he can't glance inside.

He doesn't ask if the headmaster is dead. Perhaps he knows or doesn't want to know. I hand him his vial, his name printed neatly on the glass. "We have to go."

He hurries after me down the hall, shifting back into his human body as we go, and I'm careful to always keep one hand on my bow. When we return to our room, he changes clothes, pulls on his boots, then grabs our bags.

"There's one last thing I have to do," I say quickly, dropping the bow onto my bed. Elias will have lost his material form; I can only hope he finished eating. "I'll need your help with this."

I throw back the carpet and reveal the teleportation

circle beneath. Hadrian takes my hand. "Tell me where to look," he says, forever earnest.

I pull him gently towards where the last three runes will need to be placed. The spell's draw on my body—his body—will be immense, but he's made his choice, and I've made mine.

"Watch," I whisper, and using the last of the rune paint on my desk, I finish the circle.

In response, the runes on my shoulders and upper arms glow gold, just like the runes on Hadrian's chest. He staggers back, gasping, but keeps hold of my hand. All the lines of the circle come alight, glimmering like stardust.

Reaching into the pouch on my hip, I pull out the two Frostborro phantoms I'd trapped and uncork their vials with my teeth. I think of the letters from their families, which I've decided to leave behind. I don't need the reminder; I'll always remember what they said.

"Be free," I whisper, and the phantoms enter the circle. They vanish.

There's no sense of something pulling on me, no flash or sound, no moment where they both dissolve. They simply pass behind a veil and are gone.

Letting go of Hadrian, I take out the vial of my blood and splash it across the flagstones, watching as the red smears through the paint, killing the magic. I take a rag and wipe it through the runes, leaving a mess of washed-out lines and blurry shapes. There's nothing left here for anyone to learn.

Hadrian watches me from across the room, the runes on his chest flat and dull. I save those for last and wipe them away with a tenderness I've lent few other things in all my life.

Taking Hadrian's hand again, we run down the hall. There's a loud commotion coming from up the stairwell, but the doors at the front of the academy are always unlocked, and the outer wall has no gate. When no one can leave, under threat of death, why waste time preventing someone from trying?

Outside, I can see the edge of the isle coming rapidly towards us, the grass and dirt giving way suddenly to a sharp drop.

I've looked over this edge only a few times before, just to watch the slow bob of a gondola heading our way. There's no gondola coming for us today.

"What's the plan?" Hadrian asks me, and I squeeze his hand. His voice is shaking as much as his body.

"Do you trust me?" I ask him. This is it. We'll either live or we'll die.

Hadrian nods.

"Then jump."

I pull him after me, and Hadrian follows. The fall is straight down between all four of the floating isles.

The taste of the sea rises to meet us, the wind howling past our ears. If we strike the water from this height, it will obliterate us.

My bow is still strung, the wood bent around my chest again, the string across my back. With one hand holding Hadrian, the other grabs the bow.

Elias appears, his monstrous form unchanged from earlier. He looks even less human in the bald light of dawn.

"Save us," I tell him.

He laughs.

The fall is stretching on and on, the cold so sheer I can't feel my exposed skin. I can see the water getting closer and closer. Hadrian looks like he's waiting for a miracle, his yells swallowed by the violence of the wind, his hair whipping and snapping behind him.

He can't hear me over his terror.

I shout, "Elias! You have no choice!"

If I die in the sea, the bow will sink to the sand far below, the wood decaying into mulch.

His laugh is self-defeating. "Alright, boy," he says. "You win."

My name is Pella.

His transformation is instantaneous. His long limbs melt into part of his wings, skeletal bones become flesh and feathers. He's unbelievably massive, blocking out the sky, with talons large enough to shred clifftops.

He grabs me—only me—but I'm holding Hadrian tightly enough that he's caught in the attempt. Hadrian yelps, unaware of what's happening.

Elias uses our momentum to swing us up into the air, killing the speed of our fall.

After he lets us go, we hit the water what feels like mere seconds later—and survive.

I break the surface, gasping and cold, a wave of seawater filling my mouth and nose. Hadrian is the stronger swimmer but takes longer to appear. When he does, he drags air back into his lungs, his face alight with relief.

"How the fuck did you do that?" he asks, elation making him giddy. He treads water easily, the tide pushing us both towards the island beneath the academy, towards the dock and the harbour and the waiting ship.

A sack of gold will ensure our passage to the continent. Everything has worked out as it should.

I look up at the sun. "I'm the greatest mage of our generation, aren't I?" I ask, breathless and sure. "I can do *anything*."

ACKNOWLEDGMENTS

For a book I wrote in a whirlwind over three days, it took me almost a year to edit. But here we are! Inspired by the short story I wrote in *A Chronicle of Monsters* (*To Cage a Godkiller*), *The Phantom Keeper* speaks to a very personal journey of mine, and I'm grateful to everyone who lent me their support.

To Nick: who encouraged me to write again.

To Julia: who read the first, second, and third draft with enthusiasm.

To Oana: who designed the gorgeous cover and chapter headers.

To Svifian8: who brought Pella and Hadrian to life in the perfect illustration.

To Leslie: who turned my words into the book you now hold in your hands.

And finally, to my family, but especially to my mother and my brother, Matthew: who believe in everything I do.

Thank you all.

ABOUT THE AUTHOR

Amanda Ferreira works in publishing, as an editor. She lives in Toronto with her son and her tuxedo cat, Milo, and when not writing, can be found baking, running, listening to a true crime podcast, or working on a cosplay.

Connect with her on Twitter/X (@amandatferreira) or Instagram (@aferreirawrites) for updates on her next book.